Mona came out of her clothes and right there in the middle of the room, in her bright red bikini panties, started shimmering like a bowl of jello. "Dis da way we do in Tahiti, where I come from."

We were slipping farther and farther away from the shore; lascivious behavior started a lava flow. Ingrid came out of another bag. She had studied gymnastics and ballet and came at us walking on her hands, upside down.

"Looks like now's the time," he said in a low voice. We allowed them to undress us before we joined them. Ingrid was the only one who could walk on her hands, but we could all dance, slowly, sensually. We made love; strokes being halted in midstream while waiting for a punchline.

"See how much fun this is? Lots of people take this shit too seriously, you know," my father said.

MY MENFRIENDS

ODIE HAWKINS

An Original Holloway House Edition
HOLLOWAY HOUSE PUBLISHING CO.
LOS ANGELES, CALIFORNIA

Published by
HOLLOWAY HOUSE PUBLISHING COMPANY
8060 Melrose Avenue, Los Angeles, CA 90046
International Standard Book Number 0-87067-326-2
Printed in the United States of America
Cover Illustration by Glen Tarnowski
Cover Design by Jeff Renfro

Dedicated To:
The Spirit Capoeira

Prologue

To the friends who have been written over and in, and to the ones who were not, I'd like to paraphrase some remarks.

It has always been the custom for those who want to gain the favor of a friend to do so by offering gifts which they think are the most valuable, or in which they know a friend will take special delight.

In this way friends are often presented with cars, clothes, gems, wine, beautiful, and intelligent women, and other things.

In my desire, however, to offer my friends a humble testimony of my love and good will, I have been unable to find anything among my possessions which I hold so dear or esteem so highly as the knowledge I have of my friends, gained from a constant study of their habits and attitudes.

I have diligently scrutinized their actions, and, herein, I offer the results of those observations.

Although I consider this work to be unworthy of my friends acceptance, I know that my confidence in their sense of fair play assures me that they will eventually receive the work in the light that it was written; honestly.

I haven't sought to decorate the work with long, complicated phrases or high sounding words or any of those other superficial attractions that another writer would have used to embellish his stuff.

I don't want novelties and tricks to obscure the weight that I think my menfriends deserve.

Nor would I like to have it misunderstood, or considered presumptuous on the part of someone as low on the pole as I am, that these paragraphs and sentences are attempts to reroute the affairs of my friends.

No, none of that.

In the same way that artists have always stationed themselves in the valleys in order to draw mountains, or hiked up the mountain to take a peek at the plains; this is what I have tried to do.

I pray that my menfriends will accept this in the spirit that it is offered, and if they choose to read it, will recognize my great desire to see them continue to reap the good fortune that their lives deserve.

Chapter 1

Even at thirteen, fourteen, and fifteen, we were much too individualistic to be called a gang; BoBo, Burkes, Leo (sometimes, when into imaginative self-hatred, alias Tony De Medrow) Billy Woods, Herb Cross, Bruce, Mooney, Johnny Fox, Bernard Kelly and a few others who lived in the same neighborhood and hung out on the same corners.

Some of the less informed thought we were a "gang" because we spent a lot of time together, but that was a result of them being unable to penetrate the esoteric haze surrounding our relationships.

There were times, to be honest, when we didn't really know what was happenin' either. We stood on the corners rappin' and signifyin' ("you know what, man, yo' momma is so ugly she can't even catch a cold") 'n do'wappin' ("wop doo-dooo/doo doo doo *doo* wop doo ddooo") and strengthening each other and the bonds between us without fully realizing that we were doing that, or why.

BoBo, for example, could build a lot of strength in you. BoBo, a close second to the late Nat "King" Cole in appearence, but much shorter, stockier, with tree trunk legs that were bent from the pelvis to the ankle. Yeahhh, BoBo could build a bunch of strength in you.

How much did he weigh? Hundred 'n fifty five, fifty eight? and, at the time, all ghetto hardened muscle.

Yeahhh, BoBo could build a bunch of strength in you. One of the ways he did it was to hit on you. Physically, not romantically.

We had a lil' macho number that Bo' loved. There was no official name for it. It could've been called, satirically, "shouldering a load" or "takin' it from brother Bo' " or something like that.

Yeahhh, BoBo could build a heap of strength in you, if you weren't afraid of having your arms beaten into their shoulder sockets.

No, we didn't have on an official name for it, but that didn't mean anything because, deep down, we all knew it was a survival of the fittest game and the rules were simple.

What we did was this; a group would form a circle, two people would get into the center of the circle and punch on each other's shoulders until one of them quit. The unwritten rules of the game were that you should only punch the shoulders.

There was no referee and no penalties for missing t shoulder and punching the jaw, like, there was no one on t sidelines who'd wave a red flag and say, "Yeh! that's a j shot! You just fouled that man!"

No, none of those nice things happened. One had to careful and keep a stiff jab out front.

We *were* taking our aggressions out on each other. Bo did it spectacularly, maybe he had more hostility than the r

10

of us, or whatever. He was probably the hardest hitting middleweight on the Southside, at that point in time, and there were some hard hitters around.

BoBo performed knockouts on shoulders. We had days when everybody's shoulders were semi-narcotized from BoBo's hammer hands. The brother absolutely loved to punch. And he could take one too.

We leave the circle for a moment. Someone told BoBo that this man down at the stickhall (it was never called anything but the stickhall) had been harassing his older brother (a known junky) and what was he going to do about it?

Me and somebody else trailed him to the stickhall, just to see what was going to go down. Never one to waste words, he stomped in, asked, "Which one o' you motherfuckers been fuckin' with my brother?"

"Who in the fuck is your brother?"

"James Lee."

In the midst of the sly looks, hip, undercurrent laughter and stuff, this deep, deep voice says, "I guess I'm the one you want. I stuffed my boot in that little bastard's ass, jus' the way I'm gon' do you, if you don't get the fuck outta here."

BoBo couldn't've been older than fifteen. The man was at least thirty, rockhard from the prison iron yard, nasty, mean, big.

BoBo tore his ass up. It seems that all of the frustration he had been holding in boxing us to death on the shoulders, came out. He tore the dude's ass up.

I'm sure he knocked him out about three times before he let him fall, and then speared him with a trio of left jabs before he hit the floor.

It was, to coin a cliche, awesome.

Yeahhh, the brother loved to punch. And he loved to drink that chemical shit they pour down our throats in the ghetto.

And he had fierce dreams, in addition to punching power.

Some balmy summer Southside evenings, after we had boxed, played baseball, talked cliched shit to the neighborhood sex pots, smoked a couple joints and done a half dozen other non-productive things, we'd sit on the strip of greenery that paralleled South Parkway (King Drive now) drinking this chemical mixture and talking about Europe.

Europe was the scene for us, because our fathers, uncles, brothers and friends had been over there. Asia meant the Royal Canton Cafe and Africa was only a pork chop outline in a geography book. And besides they didn't have big time blondes like the ones we saw in the movies.

"Yeahhh, man, France got to be a hip place. You heard 'Zulu' last night, didn't you? Talkin' about them French broads givin' him money 'n shit."

"Bird went over there. Yeahhh, Bird went over there and they dug the fuck outta him. Miles 'n Diz too. Can't be too bad if they dig Miles, Diz and Bird."

BoBo also took pride in speaking a lil' Spanish (I think he picked it up from a Mexican busboy, during a three day sentence as a pearldiver) and knew something about the nature of philosophical thought.

"Fuck it! It ain't 'bout nothin'!" That's a statement he would make when he was dealing with the core of something too deep for any of us to cope with, like, what is Death? or what is Life, really?

I'm sure I wasn't the only one to ask him during those days when our shoulders were throbbing from the pain (one dude, a recent addition, actually fainted once), "Bo, you ever think about boxin' for a livin'?"

"Shit! Not if I have to stop drinkin' this good pluck and smokin' this good smoke."

Years later, after we had Diaspored, strolling through a section of Washington Park where we used to take girls for heavyweight kissin'/feelin' sessions, I spotted BoBo sprawled at the base of the tree.

He was snoring softly, an empty wine bottle leaning drunkenly against the tree, flies buzzed around his wine sweetened lips.

BoBo. I stood over him for a few minutes, both shoulders suddenly aching from his remembered sledgehammer shots, undecided about waking him or not.

What if he wanted to come out of his stupor for a lil' shoulder thumping?

After watching the flab around his midsection heave and wobble for a few minutes, I decided to leave him alone.

I strolled away feeling sad about him, for him, for a few minutes, my shoulders throbbing. I looked back at him and laughed out loud.

How could you feel sorry for a motherfucker who could hit so hard you felt it twenty five years later?

I "loved" R.B. and I think he "loved" me too but we didn't know how to do anything about it. We didn't know how to do anything constructive, that is.

On most afternoons, after school, we'd race to one of the nearby alleys, position ourselves within throwing-range from each other and proceed to throw bottles (there were, literally, thousands of wine bottles, beer bottles, and milk bottles scattered around) at each other; and when the wine and beer bottles evaded easy reach, we threw half house bricks and roughed out cobblestones, "alley apples."

It's hard to figure out how we escaped serious injuries; as a matter of fact I don't remember anybody being injured at all. Miracles do exist.

And we finished that section of our "courtship," we'd stroll through a common fork in the alley, as though nothing had gone down.

I stare backward through the shattered glass, the sun flickering off on missile-bottles, the water splattering off the beer bottles on the concrete; why we weren't blinded I'll never know, and the sharp crack of bricks beyond my head, and I realize that a strong sense of who I was and what I had to do kept me from becoming R.B.'s emotional peon.

He was a "Carmen" amongst us and I was extremely sensitive to his grace and style but I never allowed my admiration to dribble over, to bubble past a certain point.

(As a writing teacher at Chino Men's "Facility," for a couple years, I grew to understand what I had put myself through with R.B. I saw it happening with a couple of dudes in the joint. Thank the Orisha that I didn't meet R.B. in the joint, he would've had my nose wide open.)

I'm sure, being as peer group cruel as any member of our peer group could be, he would've used me if he had felt certain that he had a handle on the situation.

How could he have used me? Well, he probably wouldn't've asked—but told me—to suck his dick, (we already had one of those in the "Hood." Well, two, to be exact; a fat boy with juicy thick lips and a slender, middle aged man who was never seen without an umbrella. He [the Professor] was the back and bones of several movements to take the teens off the streets and down into his "youth movement basement,") nor would he have known how to pimp me.

In effect, his "game" was undeveloped, "natural." He was one of those special people; the boxers, the visual artists, exquisite transvestites, super clever dips, outrageous conmen, writers. . . .

His love-hate thang whipped through a barrage of introverted feelings. They had to be introverted because, cool as we was, nobody could give up shit. If you can dig where I'm comin' from. . . .

We might be having a great time together, duckin' 'n dodgin' "Two Gun Pete's" boottips, spending an hour in the Virginia

14

Theatre, absorbing the funk and stank of three hundred movie enslaved bodies in a one hundred body-ship, snatchin' 'n grabbin' shit that didn't belong to us, being us, just strolling eat on 43rd Street, enjoying the sawab and jawab of each others' company, until somebody else showed up, anybody.

He would immediately switch sides, mechanically, viciously, become an enemy, make fun of my haircut, or ridicule the shoes that he had just spent five paragraphs admiring. And finally, after I had bravely carried stone to my face in order to deal with the nastiness of the attack, he would wander away with the other pack members, grinning at my pain.

One evening, unable to understand it, I almost broke down and cried, I just couldn't make myself believe that he could possibly enjoy anybody else's company more than mine. I mean, after all, wasn't I reputed to be the sexiest storyteller of them all?

We grew older, of course, and stopped throwing things at each other's heads, hoping to wound our own hearts.

The years separated us (laying BoBo down for the wino count) and, more and more, I placed my feelings in perspective and started doing what I thought was important.

There were movements when I'd remember our Spring bok jousts in the projects, flipping each other around, trying to impress jaded ghetto girls. We were too close then, to try to use bottles; that had been our own, special thang.

Now, now we circled in the circle and jabbed-faked and punched. There was an element of "courtship" to that too, because we all knew that BoBo was the boss stud in that respect.

But we did the best we could with what we could arrange. We talked about each other's mommas for a minute and had to stop that; my tongue was too quick for his family tree. I called the truce, to prevent the wounded stare from bleeding out at me, the glistening look that provoked tears inside my psyche.

We danced, he grabbed hold of this sister who had had polio sometime before she was a teenager, that had left her with a slightly withered left leg.

My girl was shapely and healthy but had no imagination. I danced behind them at the "Peps," following his dips and her swirls. It was like the Dance Theatre of Harlem fo'real.

The drift carried us to far corners.

Years later, on 63rd Street, near King Drive, I was returning from a European vacation; I ran into R.B.

We postured for a bit, I felt my skin grow clammy, remembering some of the changes he used to take me through. I wondered if someone else would trip through and make him do a number on me. Or would I allow that to happen?

"Where you been man, ain't seen you in a long time?"

"Well, I been traveling a lot, Mexico, Europe..."

"Oh yeah, you must be rich now, huh?"

"Naw, not rich, just doin' my thang."

We paused to do a lil' simultaneous flirting with a couple passing "Moments," enchanting us with cheap perfume and Solid Gold sway-motions.

"Just doin' your thang, huh?"

"Yeahhhh, just doin' my thang. What's happenin' with you?"

For a glittering moment, my soul bent, watching the wounded fawn look in his eyes, the place my face always settled on, fixated on pain and beauty, the two elements my heart always cried for in the ghetto.

"Oh, well, you know how it be; I be doin' a lil' this 'n a lil' that."

"Ummmmm huh."

It was all over, I was cold cocked now, my hat cooled, the ferocious hormones controlled and channelled. This motherfucker was not about shit and had never been.

16

He hadn't changed much, except for the fact that he had always been one, psychologically, in the way that junkies are born and not made, and I had never realized it. Not up 'til now, at any rate.

No, he hadn't changed much, except for the fact that he was a fo'real, bona fide dope fiend, black-belt level 10th (that's when you steal from your momma and lie on your friends).

"Uhhh, dig, man, why don't you loan me ten dollars 'til tomorrow?"

"When you gon' pay me back?"

"When? C'mon thru tomorrow 'bout this same time."

"Tomorrow about this same time, huh?"

"Yeahhh, 'bout this same time."

"Yeahhh."

"Sounds like I've heard that before."

"Huh?"

"Nothin'; forget it. Here's twenty man. Take it easy."

No, he hadn't changed much, except for the fact that he was a junky.

A few blocks away, suckin' on a nervous, solitary drink, I could understand why he'd been shootin' heroin. He'd always been stuck on himself, but that was one of the peculiar qualities that made him who he was.

Herb. Sometimes I picture Herb as a Sumo Man, not simply in terms of bulk, but as a creature who has always been there, a pre-historic Man, in a sense.

I deliberately capitalize Man when referring to him because he has always been a Man. When we were younger, he always seemed to be older, not in looks but in the way he made decisions, or provisions for circumstances that most of us didn't even think about taking seriously.

For example, girls. We were out there trying to collect as many labial sporans (or cunts, to be Angloid about it) while

Herb seemed to be looking for a wife.

"I want somebody to feed my gut and pat my butt."

As a teenager, the oldest son in a large family, he worked as a waiter in an exclusive hotel in Evanston, Illinois, which meant that in our poverty stricken neck of the ghetto he had money, tips, bread, all the time.

And he shared. Willie Tobias, Bernard Kelly and I had many a feast at the Royal Canton Cafe, hosted by Herb.

He shared. I really started looking at that trait superhard, after we became adults. It seemed to me that his kharma was constantly renewing goodies for him and the only conclusion I could reach is that his giving was allowing him to receive more.

The best friend an artist could ever have. He did not/may not read the latest novels, or hmmm and stroke his chin in front of the latest painting, but he obviously realized many years ago, that none of the hmmmms and chin strokes would keep the wrinkles out of the artist's belly.

He has fed this artist often, nurtured his soul with profoundly philosophical statements and maintained his balance over the course of a number of rocky trips.

He has often reminded me, just by being there, of where we came from and the lush romanticism of those times, that couldn't be stifled by the ugliness of the life around.

"Hawk, you 'member that time me, you, BoBo, Bernard Kelly and somebody else was sittin' out there on the middle divider on South Park, drinkin' wine, talkin' about going to Europe 'n stuff?"

"Yeah, I remember that."

"I thought about that one day when I was in Paris, strollin' down the Champs Elysee. I had a beret on. My partner Barbie had scored for some morphine tablets and I was high as I could be, feeling no pain. I don't know why but for some reason I thought about that time, well, a whole bunch of times

18

like that."

"I know what you mean, man, it crossed my mind a lot too, when I was in Spain."

He has always shared.

"C'mon in, baby, grab a plate! Get yourself a drink, you know where it is."

I'd like to write a perfect story for him someday, something he wouldn't have to spend time reading, but that he could hold in his hands and inform him vibrationally, that his barbeque, gin, sensible gifts and excellent company were the catalyst for something very special.

My menfriends started off being boys and it was at that stage of the metamorphical process that I knew most of them; others drifted through later, their shells formed and collated.

The brothers from Bowen Avenue on the Southside of Chicago; BoBo, R.B., Herb, Mooney, Sherman, Leo, a.k.a., (when he was going through his other identities) Tony De Medrow or Antonio Tango. Or whatever the moment called for.

We spent a rainy afternoon speaking quasi-Spanish, Leo/Tony and me, to each other, in front of a couple impressionable females who probably thought we were nuts. But, let's face it, they didn't know us well. We were *nuts*.

There were times, stroked by a wild hair or two, when it seems that we would do anything.

Check it out: one afternoon me and Herb were just patrolling the neighborhood, searching for foreign piss stains. We came across several of his younger brothers and a few other younger dudes hanging around the basement entrance to someone's apartment.

We checked the scene out from across the street. They were going in and out at regular intervals, zipping their flies and exchanging sly grins.

What the hell was goin' on here?!

We went over and rousted them from the set.

"What the fuck you young motherfuckers doin'? Git the fuck away from here 'fore we stick boot in yo' asses!"

"Awww, c'mon, y'all sho' is rotten!"

"You heard what I said—git yo' ass in gear!"

I can only assume that the last zipper had been re-zipped as the only reason for them not putting up a real fight.

They slouched away, grumbling revenge fully. We opened the raggedy screen door and stopped into something that looked like an abstract stage setting.

Bare room, a chair, a bed under a bald light bulb dangling by a black cord, a slender naked brown skinned girl ironing a few yards from the bed, semen oozing from her crotch.

We stared at her for a few beats, trying to figure something out.

She tilted the iron up and gracefully laid down on the bed, her legs jackknifed in the air. When my turn came I looked into two eyes that gleamed like marbles. Her womb had been hollowed out, their shores widened beyond my physical capabilities. There was nothing to do but explode and go.

We were halfway down the block, sneaking a peripheral peek at the return of the younger dudes, a few new faces in the group, before words could come.

"Damn! She must be a nymph!" Herb exclaimed.

I was glad he had found a name for her, I was flirting with half a dozen names, one of them was Sirena.

I think about that young girl sometimes, she was my introduction to nymphomania.

Yeahhh, we were nuts, wandering through nutty situations. Madness.

Billy Woods, the wiry brown brother with the hollow cheeks who was officially known as "Long Dick Woods."

We talked about Billy's penis often; clinically, objectively, as though it were a tree branch. Or a tributary flowing off the Mississippi.

There were times, in a detached manner, as we pissed up and down the alleys, he would spool his member out and allow us to make up-to-date surreptitious measurements.

Penile envy never played in our relationships; Billy Woods cancelled that particular monster out by being on the scene.

Strangely, there was no arrogance attached to his Olympian dimensions. He was "Long Dick Woods" to himself and to us, and that was that. No head trips.

Funny thing happened once, in connection to Billy; it had to do with me becoming friendly with and the lover of a woman who had once been Billy's lover; once.

She didn't know that I had grown up with him and, for awhile, I didn't know that she had known him or under what circumstances.

We were about to do what we usually did on Wednesday night (sometimes Tuesday, if the vibes dropped down heavy), after the children had been prodded off to sleep (I think she had four. Was one of them "Long Dicks"?) but somehow got sideswiped. The foreplay had taken us to a verbal level (a place she confessed she'd never been). The verbiage throbbed back and forth for a few beats and wound up, who knows why or how? on his holy name.

"Billy Woods, 'Long Dick'?. . ."You know him?"

"Hmf! Shit! I grew up on the same street with him."

Passion surrendered to toasts to his memory and a story from an honest woman.

"We was workin' at this laundry together, not the place I'm at now, another one. Anyway, in comes this real slender dude. Did he ever gain any weight?"

"He hadn't the last time I saw him."

"That's good. Damn, wish I could lose some of these rubber tires I got 'round my. . . ."

21

"What happened?"

"You really wanna hear this?"

"You motherfuckin' right I wanna hear, you talkin' 'bout one of my partners."

"O.K., well, anyway, you know how he was about women. Is he still that way?"

"I ain't seen him in awhile."

"Well, anyway. . . ."

I cradled my left hand behind my head, balanced my third tumbler of Jack Daniels on my chest and settled back to listen to a "Long Dick" story from another side of the sexual tracks.

"He actually hit on my girlfriend, Esther, first. The way she told it to me was like he just came right up to her and asked her for some."

I almost spilled my drink laughing. The brother was *known* to be direct. The way he put it, feeling philosophical one day, "Fuck! I don't give a damn! If they say yes or no, the important thing is to ask 'em. Lots broads don't ever get asked. Including superfine broads, they got pussies 'n assholes too."

"Well, to make a long story short, she said no. I asked her why she said, 'No.' I mean, she had already told me she thought he was cute 'n everything."

Long Dick Woods cute?!

I swallowed a big sip of my Jack. "Long Dick", cute?? Hmmm, obviously we were approaching the brother's sexual attraction from another side of the facet, another perspective altogether.

"I thought she was stupid to turn him down just because he came right on out and said, 'You wanna gimme some?' Don't you think that was stupid?"

I refreshed her drink and thoughtfully nodded in agreement. She pinched my thigh affectionately.

"I *know* you think it was stupid. So, anyway, a couple days later he was pushin' a gurney fulla dirty shirts past my station and he leaned over and popped the question in my ear."

"And you said yes?"

"Well, not right then. I told him I'd give him my answer after lunch. That's when I gave him a semi-yes. We got off work at 5:30 and he took me out to this lil' ol' bar near the 'El'."

"The Club Biscayne?"

"Club Biscain? Yeah, I think that's what it was called, right near the 'El' on 55th Street?"

"Uhh huh."

"Anyway, we had a few drinks; he talked a lotta crazy shit to me and then we left there and went to this motel over on Stoney Island."

The Starlite? Probably the Dew Bop. He *would* take her there.

"Place had mirrors all over the walls 'n stuff. Kinda fancy. I could tell he knew his way around. We sat on the side of the bed 'n started kissin' 'n what not, so I suggested that, instead of wrinklin' my skirt up 'n what not, why not just get on in the bed 'cause that's what we had come for. I see you smilin'. . . .

"Can't help it, baby, I just can't help it."

She took a long pull on her drink, her eyes beginning to glitter with memories.

"Well, hey, you know the way I am. If I get hot I'm just hot and that's that. I guess that's why I had these babies so fast 'fore I had my tubes tied."

I sloshed another slug of Jack in my tumbler and tipped a hook in hers.

"O.K., so, I just pull my skirt off 'n my blouse, bra 'n panties 'n get in bed. 'Well?' I asked him, 'What're you gonna do? He didn't say anything for a couple minutes and then he started undressin'.

He pulled his shoes 'n socks off, took his shirt off, took

23

his pants off and started peelin' his drawers down. That's when I got shook. I was lookin' at him from all these angles in these mirrors and, at first, I thought I was seein' some kind of oplical ellusion...."

"You mean optical illusion."

"Yeah, that's what I said, that's what I thought I was seein'. It was like an elephant trunk comin' out of his drawers. I'm not gonna lie, I was scared. I was too scared to move. Ohhh nooo, you ain't gon' put that...that...that in me. No Sirree.

"He smiled real smooth like and said, real sweet—'O.K., just the head. That's all, O.K.?'"

We both laughed so hard I thought we were going to wake the children up.

"The head?! Shit! By the time he got thru wormin' half that pipe up into me I was damned near paralized. I couldn't move. We just laid there for a few minutes and he's tellin' me, real smooth like, 'See, that ain't too bad, is it? I just got the head in.'"

I backflashed on the scene. We had only seen a semi-piss hard type erection during our wine alley wine-beer-piss-sessions I tried to visualize this thing she was talking about, fully erect.

The thought defeated my imagination.

"I'm not gonna lie to you, by the time he got half of this...this...where in the world did he get a thang like that anyway?! Was his father built like that?"

Hmmmm...Mr. Woods? A slightly larger frame but was he built like that? Was it hereditary? His brothers weren't built like that. Maybe he was a mutation.

"Uhhh, I don't know, sweetheart. I never saw that part of his ol' man."

"I was just wonderin'. The thang had a bend in it. Like a bow 'n arrow, you know like a bow."

Incredible. A woman's perspective. We never saw that sec-

24

tion of the pipe.

"My girlfriend asked me the next day, she had seen us cut out together, what did y'all do last night? I didn't evey try to tell 'er."

An unfamiliar feeling quietly started draining down from my head to groin. Was it jealousy? Emma gently clutched my flaccid joint.

"This ain't messin' with you, is it?"

"Messin' with me, ohh no, I'm cool." Was I?

"Anyway, all I got to say is that boy had a helluva good time finder on him. He used to try to get me to go out with him again but I told him—straight out—no, baby! I can't afford no female trouble right in through here. He did manage to finally persuade Esther to go out with him.

"She showed up the next day walkin' lap legged, with her eyes all bugged out 'n what not. It took her a few months to describe, to confess that she had given the brother a lil' head but she didn't know what she was doin' 'cause he had kept the light off.

"Yes indeed, honey, that Billy Woods had an elephant trunk 'tween his legs. I remember once. . . ."

Funny, nobody ever said, "Big Dick," they always said, "Long Dick." Wonder where "Long Dick" is these days?

Chapter 2

Dicky was a boyhood friend who should be a great man now, if he survived the Westside. I'm trippin' back quite a bit now, back to when winters were warmer and summers were not quite so hot.

We lived on Washburne Avenue, one block south of Roosevelt Road, down the street from each other. My clan lived in a basement that flushed sewer water thru the place when the snow melted. He lived with his sisters and brothers, in a rickety house on stilts that had missing planks in the floor. We were not well off, as they say.

In my memory-frame, Dicky was a summer time friend, someone I shared the heat, humidity, buzzing flies, ghetto sunshine, garbage ridden alleys and stolen watermelon with.

He was usually the person I started my mornings and ended my evenings with, roaming through the South Water Market in the mornings to pick up cabbages, bruised tomatoes, busted melons of all kinds and, from time to time, a sack of potatoes.

Evenings, we stalked lion and tiger-rats in the alleys with broomstick spears; very effective with large nails driven into the end.

Dicky was deadly with the "spear," the half house brick. He could also throw a butcher knife pretty well too.

"What do they talk about?" I overheard one of my cousins ask one day.

"Who knows?" the other one answered.

I was puzzled by the question, at that time; I mean, shit, we talked about whatever twelve year old dudes talked about.

It didn't matter that Dicky couldn't speak real words because he could describe stuff, using his eyes, his body, his fingers so well that you'd have to be an idiot *not* to know what he was saying.

He was a fantastic mime.

Although I never asked him, I always assumed that the large crater of proud flesh on the left side of his pepper-corned noggin had something to do with him not being able to speak normally.

Dicky's "speech" pattern was musical, lilting, complex. Sometimes he sounded like a wounded duck. When he was feeling good and had a lot to say he gave hints of being John Coltrane's soprano saxophone.

When he really wanted to pull you into something fairly complicated, he would mime-dance it out.

During the years I knew him he always seemed to disappear in September, when school started. I don't think he was being sent to a school for the speech impaired or anything that civilized. I think he simply avoided the whole issue of school. And yet, fantastically, he could read. I have no idea how he learned, but he could.

One afternoon, as I was trekking through one of our favorite alley-trails, my head busting open from a day of academic

28

hammering, he picked up my spoor, clamped his arm around my head (one of our friendliest greeting-gestures) and grabbed one of my books and started reading it.

What the hell was it? What kind of dumb, irrelevant crap did they have us reading 'way back then? I don't remember, but I'll never forget his reading.

I leaned against a telephone post and reviewed the performance.

He was the old grandmother with the shawl on her head, the brother and sister lost in the Magic Forest, the wood-chopper hunting the naughty wolf, the joyful population of the town called Moneville. I applauded and laughed until tears came.

In my dreams, since those hellified days, I've often imagined the two of us floating through sun drenched alleys piled with exotic garbage.

He is "telling me, just as he used to do, a story that has six or seven characters and takes place on foreign soil (maybe Oak Street on the Near Northside), he even indicates their size, weight, age and tonal complexities and yet, not a word is spoken.

Dicky was one of the most intriguing storyteller-conversationalists I've ever known. The first time I saw Marcel Marceau, I sat there smirking, thinking: Marcel baby, you got a long way to go to get to where Dicky was.

Mooney, Sherman, Leo. They were a part of the Bowen Street "gang" and its only right that I should come back up on them in this way. This is the way it was always happening with us.

The last time I saw Mooney, he was making his grand-badfooted-stroll across 43rd and King Drive. I was just doing the nostalgia bit on a three week trip back into my roots.

"Odee; go back man, git off the scene, it ain't the way it was when we was growin' up 'round here, this shit done got serious."

The way it was when we was growin' up 'round there. . . .

Sports, reefer smokin' cheap wine drinkin', sports, promiscuous sexual behavior; lots of perversions were going on but the dangers (gang warfare, Uzi drive by shootings, cocaine turf disputes, etc.,) were nonexistent.

Sports. Everybody had to play everything, it was a peer group law. All of the five foot five people became fire eating basketball guards, all of the lean became runners, everybody played baseball, football and handball.

Mooney was a reluctant football player. He was five eight or so, 140 pounds, at fourteen, exactly the right size for a split end. But he didn't like football. He didn't seem to care too much for baseball either, and handball was simply an obstacle to boredom.

Mooney was a boxer. Strangely, I recall him blinking and ducking and almost cowering on the football field, obviously dying for the sun to go down so that he could get away from all the brutality of this Neanderthal collectivist madness.

He carried none of those emotions into the ring. When he popped between the ropes at the gym over there on 51st Street and Indiana, out of the 'hood, it was like watching a fish swim.

He was struck in the Sugar Ray mold; not Leonard, Robinson. His dance backwards (even after a night of Charlie Parker listenin', reefer smokin' 'n cheap wine drinkin') was brilliantly evasive and when he suddenly paused to jack off a dozen jabs with both hands, the effect could only be termed a ballet of hands.

On some occasions, very seldom to be sure, he and BoBo would get down. There was never a lot of damage done because they had too much respect for each other.

There was no need to throw big punches or clinch for maximum body thumping. They circled and flicked counter flicks at each other. It was almost a kind of fistic Capoeira.

BoBo would shuffle to the right, to position himself for the right hook. Mooney would duck-dance to the left, to avoid the right hand attack and set himself up to deliver one of his "Afro-Cuban punches," he called them.

If their stuff was working to the max, they could shuffle and dance for five minutes without a full punch or jab being thrown. The effect was almost hypnotic, like watching two mongooses play tag with each other.

And when it was over, that or whatever, we'd retire to the alley for a...ahemm..."cocktail" or two. Or three. Or four.

That seemed to be Mooney's biggest problem, "The cocktail hour." He never did a full BoBo, but, even after he had acquired a full fledged manager and an allowance, he could never give himself over fully to the gym discipline.

"Hey man, don't you have a fight on Thursday?"

"Yeahhh, you got that right, buddy, and I'm gon' punch that sucker into next week. Pass me the joint, please suh."

And he did that. He kicked asses and took names but he would never train hard or seriously enough to kick major league asses or take major league names.

When he said, "Go back, things ain't like they used to be;" I knew that I should listen, no one knew better than Mooney, about time warps and abstract rhythms.

Sherman was different. Sherman wasn't a BoBo, a Mooney, an R.B. or a Billy Woods. It was hard to say, it would be hard to say what Sherman was before he became a junky. I sometimes think that he was biding his time in Never Be Nobody Land until he became a dope fiend.

He was short, dark, had a big head, a distinctive face and was kind of a "blender," that is, until he became a dope fiend.

Before he became a dope fiend, the fourth brother in his family to opt for heroin, he played the games, talked the usual shit, but it was like looking at a sleep walker, someone who

31

was feeling for the window ledge they wanted to fall from.

He seemed to fall into his niche when he became a dope addict.

We were curious (nobody went Moral, it was too expensive) and quizzed him about it. One would think, after watching three brothers suck the needle. . . .

"Sherman, what happened, man?"

"Fuck you mean, what happened?"

"I mean, you know, like, after watchin' all your brothers fall 'n shit, why would you. . . .?"

"Heyyy, don't be doin' no trip on my Thang, man. Look, so 'n so is a dancer, blah we blah wee is a singer, I'm a dope fiend. O.K.? O.K.? We all got to be what we got to be, home. Ain't that the God's Truth? Why don't chew lay this dime on me so I can get my wake up?"

Johnny Fox turned his head every time he saw Sherman because his sister was also a dope fiend, and a 'hoe.

It was really rough on Fox. I didn't really realize how rough until that fatal night in deep December.

Cold December night in Chi, Santa Claus off to the bitter right, shit steamin' in doorways.

Where are we going? Or coming from? Who knows?

The weird thing about our lives, it seemed to me, is that we were so nomadic, within such a limited area.

Anyway, we're walking, hunch kneed, hands punched into pockets, trying to feel the warmth of our nuts, plunge our hands into our crotches as we walked.

We were fetuses on the move, dredging our places between the winds, fucking with a barren destiny. All this to say, it was cold as a Black Motherfucker.

The route whipped us through Calumet Avenue, between 47th and 48th, hoetime.

She said, "Y'all wanna do some bizness?" Lady lady echoes whistling past the frigid bricks and my frozen nuts.

I suddenly remembered that I had five dollars (the going rate was 3 for the 'hoe 'n two for the room, unless you wanted to go fancy). It wasn't a conscious decision, it was simply the right thing to respond to.

I pivoted toward the sound of the voice; yes, a woman, pussy. Thighs, fucking, warmth, National-Geographic-Neanderthal-Esquimo-happiness.

Lou Rawls, Brotherman, is right, it can get colder in Chicago than anywhere in the world.

"3 'n 2," she said, under half lidded eyes, and turned to go up the stairs.

It only took three steps for both of us to realize that it was his sister, the sister we all called Sister McMullan. It would've been impossible *not* to recognize her from behind because that was her signature-trademark.

The sister's face had sucked in, her titties had dribbled, her arms had ulcerated but her Kalahari body had remained the same.

I have a peripheral glance and discovered that Fox had dissolved, whistled back out into the wind, blown by shame and the moment.

I went through with it. Under the glare of a dim blue bulb, on top of a sperm splattered bedspread, I plunged my frozen dick into my friend's sister's pussy and worked myself to a climax, thinking about the fistfight we were going to have to have, because I had fucked his sister. Honor was strength in those days.

Heroically, he forgot the whole episode and went on to Junior College. I think his sister is still out there, servicing the frozen legions.

Leo was also different, but I mean, like real different.

I mentioned earlier that he was sometimes called Tony De Meddrow or Tony Tango. Or whatever the international moment called for. It wasn't easy for him to become another

33

somebody, but I guess those are the perils of redesigned identities.

I'd never been able to get off into De Laurentis' problem, or Givenchy's or Bis'tillas'; but Leo, Leo, yeahhh, I can go there. . . . Please see this tall-reed slender African-American yaller ghetto man-boy, doing a tango so sensual that some of the middle-class-ghetto school teachers (Lake Meadows, early uhh huhhhsss. . .) used to sushi-come in their Howard University panties when they danced with him.

"Leo, who in the fuck taught you how to teach people how to tango?"

"Didn't you see 'Valentino'?"

"Yeah, I saw it five times."

"Well?"

"Well, if yo' fuckin' ass wasn't so short you would've seen that it was made for a motherfucker like me."

"Hmf!"

And there he was, pausing to lay them back on their heels at the Ida B. Wells Recreation Center, "Dance Hour with Tony."

The brother was a serious success story, on many levels. He was dancing a foreign dance (the mambo, chachacha, merenge, pachanga, hoochie coochie and the tango; "Tango Tony").

"Leo?"

"Call me Tony, I gotta rehearsal today."

"Awright, Tony, what's gonna happen? How long you gon' be able to play this shit out?"

" 'Til the gold comes home, home; 'til the gold comes home."

The gold came home on a truck. He became the owner of a trucking concern (are we into poetic justice, Western style, here?) and got fat ("I eat two orders of bar-be-que, always.") and when last heard from, was on his way back

34

from Hawaii.

"You know somethin' man, them motherfuckers oughta do somethin' about them white folks stealin' their dance shit. Can you dig where I'm comin' from?"

Yeahhh, I hear you, Tony, I always did. Leap with me. . . .

Armando Peraza, an inland sea of African rhythms, self preservation in motion. Watching Armando play the congas one night at the Lighthouse, I suddenly had the impression that he had become a god. It had nothing to do with the fact that he was playing 6/8 so fast that his hands were threatening to turn into black butter, or that his eyes had unplugged from their sockets and seemed to be focusing on a point beyond everyone's head.

The god-impression wasn't even reinforced by the illusion of him levitating behind the drums, there was something else happening; that nebulous veil that incredible folks drop on you, that allows you to fix your emotional thermometer on a certain degree was happening.

He was opening the gates to Drum Heaven. And we were trippin' thru in droves; some of the women were crying as they stepped through.

Two African-American wage slaves, freed for the weekend, were rocking their heads back and forth in a sedentary dance, their neckties clenched in their teeth, their eyes closed with cosmic rage.

Several white men fainted, unable to cope with the darkness of this Paradise. It was impossible to determine how long he allowed us to remain in this place, but I'm certain that it ended at 2 a.m. because that's when the Lighthouse turned on their lights.

But like anything else, before the lights came on there was a beginning.

Anybody remember that time frame when African-Americans on the Southside used to go to do the mambo on Tuesdays at McKies?; the mambo and cha cha cha on Wednesdays at Budland?; the pachanga and meregue on Thursdays at The Bar? Friday and Saturday might open up new floors to be stroked.

Non-Spanish speakers chanted out the choruses to "Anabacoa" and "Coco Seco" as though they spent the last century in the Jesus Maria district of La Habana. The scene was hot with Afro-Cuban-Puerto Rican-Brasilian-Venezuelan-Vera Cruz music.

"The Peps," on 47th, near St. Lawrence, used to become an Afro-Cubano Kharmic barrio on some weekends.

And into the middle of all this steps Armando Peraza. Well, actually, he wasn't stepping into anything, he was already there. I did the stepping.

Hot night on the Southside, humid, rank with sexual suggestiveness. One of those nights when all Black women get oily and become queens. One of those kinds of evenings.

Me, just prowling the turf, watching the bright colors and absorbing the rhythms. The Trianon was a dance palace that I'd never been in. I had stood outside, watching the Finian Rainbow go in a couple years; the "Finians" were those gorgeously spaced out impersonators who drove up in Benz's, Bo'hams, pink Hogs 'n the Like, gently touching the brazen arms of their proud escorts, once a year. But I'd never been inside.

I stood off to one side watching a parade of beautiful black people trip inside the Trianon (beautiful black people, meaning that some of them were ivory shaded) and, after a few couples, discovered that I couldn't really figure out what they were saying.

Tito Puente was doing timbales and Peraza was fingering the bongos like two round pianos. We had been listening to the music, we'd been dancing to the music but we hadn't checked it out live.

He sat on a chair near the stage apron, making castanet actions on the bongos. I wandered thru the crowd, drawn by this small Afro-Cuban brother.

I'd never seen anyone that proud. The pride was what you noticed first, the Earth One signal that asked, "Am I not unique? Is not this a special Something that I'm doing?"

Sugar Ray Robinson had it, Manolete, Pelé, Rizidinha, Paul Robeson, Bob Marley, Babatunde Olatunji, Richard Pryor in his salad days, a few others...Armando Peraza.

I stood, mesmerized, at the lip of the stage; he was decent to me. He didn't give the put down look that a lot of horn players might've given. Or some of the other ultra hipsters might've laid on me. He smiled at my reactions and, during one wonderful roll that lasted five minutes, he threw his head back and laughed, his front tooth sparkling with a fleck of gold at the chipped edge.

There was nothing to say after the applause, nothing to do but begin to collect his art. I discovered him placing so many rhythmic possibilities behind George Shearing for eleven years that it dawned on me why George Shearing had become George Shearing.

In between coming to know whenever his solo was going to happen on each cut, I moved to California. He, like all musicians, went to Japan, Florida, Spain, Germany, Scotland and elsewhere.

We checked back into each other in California; he was with Cal Tjader, furnishing a vertebrae that Tjader was smart enough to supply himself with (Carlos "Patato" Valdez, Mongo, Julito Collazo, Papaito, Willie BoBo, Orestes Vilato, Francisco Aguabello, Luis Kant, Chocolate, etc.).

It would've been impossible to ignore me after all the years of seeing my face in the first row.

He was the star of the Tjader ensemble but that wasn't apparent to some of the Cal Tjader aficionados. It was almost painful to have to sit through three numbers that Bobby Hutcherson, Milt Jackson or even Lionel "Smiley" Hampton would've worn Cal's ass out on (don't get me wrong; yes, he *was* an excellent musician), waiting for Armando to mount the stage.

It would not be an exaggeration to say, on at least three occasions, he was "mounted" on the stage.

One evening, 'round about midnight, he had laid so much stuff out that the drums began to play themselves as he did a supernatural mambo off to the side.

We finally started dealing with each other head up. It happened while he was at the Lighthouse, once again doing the "Soul Sauce" with Tjader.

"Wait for me after the set."

I don't remember what I had to do, or what may have mattered the morning after, none of it mattered.

We ate stale slices of pie at Lococos on the beach strip and rapped. We drove back to the hotel he was staying in on the beach. And we rapped. Or rather, he rapped. And rapped.

We sat in the minute parking lot of his hotel as he rapped. His rappin' was like his drumming, filled to the brim with counterpoint complexities, simultaneous calls and self-evident responses.

He spoke about the Cuba that gave birth to the need for Castro (not the man, the emotion), the days spent carrying water to men in the cane fields for 10 cents a day!

"10 cents?! You mean....?!"

"That's what I said, my freend, 10 cents!"

When Havana was filled with Mongos and any street corner would give up a "Patato" and a "Totica," if you had the patience to listen.

Peraza set a standard for me, "El Mejor," the best, and I thank him for it.

"If you are the best, my freend, they cannot ignore you. They cannot."

I'm trying.

The Best. I'm positive that John Bloch would relocate to that, not in a Perazian way, but in his own way.

(I have to state right here that John is a white man and he is the only white man who will occur in this account, for historical and our/storical reasons.)

It was directly after the Watts Rebellion (that the bourgeous white media always calls a "riot"); the Writers Guild of America West, Inc., or should I say, a segment, discovered that they didn't have any Black writers in the organization. This was 1966.

It is now 1988 and they still have less than 3%, out of a Guild membership of something like 9,000. Oh well, progress.

In any case, the "Open Door" program was set up, obviously to let a few Ethiopians sneak through.

I wrote a short story about a West Indian G.I. who loved to drink and it qualified me to be in the program. John Bloch was the Writing Instructor.

This wasn't my first writing workshop, that obstacle had been cleared when I was in high school.

My savior, Dr. Margaret Burroughs, had turned me onto a class that was very competently led by a middle aged blonde with slightly bucked teeth.

I'm sure the class was a good one but my memory of it is hazed out; these were adults smoking very sophisticatedly (some even had little miniature skillet ashtrays) and afterwards they tripped down the street to the Grand Hotel for martinis.

From 1952-53 to 1966 is a long time between writing workshops, but I made it.

Bloch was/is a unique kind of teacher. He was able to work the livin' shit out of some of us, those who were willing to

39

do the endless re-writing that distills superior stuff.

I didn't know what to think about the dude at first; sometimes I still don't....

I wasn't into strident "black" militancy for the sake of it, so I didn't find it necessary to gobble up all his goodies in class and talk nasty about him behind his back.

I checked him out closely for a few months; he didn't make *any* patronizing statements, identified himself honestly and didn't take any shit from anybody, in a nice way.

Deep in the back of my head I'm sure I must've called him a blue-eyed motherfucker a few times, after he had placed his pinkie directly on what was faulty in one of my "masterpiece" pieces. But I realized he was forcing me to recognize how one was supposed to funnel a talent into a craft.

There were days and evenings, sitting on the sofa by the window in the lovely house up in the Canyon, when I felt that the Way was being opened for me.

I really began to like this white guy, not because he was white, but because of what we had in common. You didn't have to call him every day to maintain a strong level of friendship, or grin in his face every time you saw him, and he took it for granted that we were men in the world.

The years of patient teaching, careful nurturing, prepared my head to accept rejections as evenly as acceptances, and that is something that only someone who knows what they're doing can teach.

I'll be more than proud to hear, someday, that I've been capable of continuing the run. No blocks here....

Looser times. Weird how going forward can make you look backwards. Strange to come from people who know they are the best, to someone who really didn't know he was the best.

I really don't know why we called him "The Toe," but we did.

"The Toe" was a fellow traveler, a dude to hang out with, a brother to share the wine and beer with, to croon on the tape with, to lust after the ladies, play blast-the-court-basketball.

I think that's when I first noticed "The Toe," on the court. Here we have this short, barrel shaped brother with pop-bottle bottomed glasses, racing up and down the basketball court, dribbling around and through people, snorting when he went up for his two points.

The incongruity of this unlikely looking figure handling a basketball like a yo-yo is something that fascinated lots of people for a long time.

And he could sing. He could sing like Lou Rawls could sing, or Billy Eckstein, or Joe Williams, or Nat "King" Cole, or Arthur Prysock, or Al Hibbler, but he couldn't sing like Willie "The Toe" Tobias.

Strangest thing in the world to hear, this young blood with all of these Ancient Ages blending in his voice. There were nights when he would take his voice around to the parties (we were too young for the joints) and earn a few coins and sneak a drink, if there was anything open.

Complex dude; he had graduated from high school without fully learning how to read. Or write.

But that never prevented him from having brilliant conversations with those who wanted to have brilliant conversations with him.

If he was ever completely caught off the bag he'd space, otherwise he'd hang tough and make eloquent shrugs and monosyllabic commentary that would stick the ball back into the other guy's park.

"Now just a moment, let me get this straight; are you saying that a peripheral judgement of the East African political situation at this time is enough to justify the use of terroristical tactics?"

"Wouldn't you?"

We're not talking about ignorance here, just shrewd skill usage.

I recall, with a deep smile, the scene at a Hyde Park party (1960's, Interracial set #101). "The Toe" and I have wandered onto the scene from another scene. Or a couple other scenes.

The women, driftees from Winnetka, Evanston and Chicago's Gold Coast, all seem to be ash-blonded, be-ringed and expensively sweatered. The wine was mega-cuts above the Ripple we'd been drinking and when "The Toe" whispered, "What is this shit these people spreadin' on they crackers?" (Paté) I knew we were roaming on different grounds.

We separated briefly, lured into opposite corners by a Spanish redhead and a corn-stalked monster of a Swede, respectively.

"Heyyy, man," he circled back to me fifteen minutes later, "I got this superfine motherfucker over here in this corner. . . ."

"Yeahhhh, I can see that. What's happenin'?"

Someone had broke out ten joints of Wisconsin sinsemilla, the folksingers and Peter Seegar geetars were a half step away, the Sixties. . . .

"I don't know. That's the problem, she keeps flappin' her jaws about some shit that don't make a bitta sense to me, shit about Mox-Leanism 'n shit. What the fuck is she talkin' about?"

"Fuck if I know, but I betcha one thing, if you doubled back on her with something you knew somethin' about, that would pop her cork."

"Yeah, like what?"

"Well, like, well, what the fuck do you know something about?"

It was really touching to stand there, in the dim party bulb light, watching his brow wrinkle as he tried to figure out what he knew something about.

"Basketball?"

"Shit! Why not? What does she know about that?!"

I was so curious about what might develop I wandered away from my corner, to monitor "The Toe's" corner.

She: "And you've got to understand that Karl Marx is the father of proleterianistic thought."

He: "Oohh, so I guess you could say that he be like Shellie McMillan, huh?"

She: "Shellie MacMillan?"

He: "The best fuckin' center you ever seen, he could pivot left and fake right and put it up fallin' backwards."

She: "Oh, I see. A pivotal figure. Was he active in the labor movement?"

He: "Hey, Shellie was active on the court, you dig?"

She: "Hmm, an attorney. I can't say that I'm familiar. . . ."

He took a moment to sip his wine and double shuffled her off into the boxing ring. Was Sugar Ray Robinson really better than Mao? Or what the deal was?

"The Toe" could do that kind of stuff. He could fake left and go right. Or fake right and go left, both moves difficult to make if you've never tried them.

I had my first baby girl in his home, or rather, his parents' home (that's what apartments were called back then).

We were in the habit of pausing in his space after school, to sing a few songs into his primitive (pre-Japanese) tape recorder, sip a few surreptitious glasses of rotten beer or just talk dirty about all the girls we knew.

On this particular day I had something a bit more tangible to deal with.

"My momma might be home in a few minutes!"

"I won't be long."

The "love scene," a vivid testimony of the need for sexual sensitivity sessions in our schools, must've coasted into five

43

minutes. The ejaculation done, the sperm dazzled upwards, hormones colled out, we departed. She and I, that is. . . "The Toe" immediately set to work, straightening out the ruffled covers 'n stuff.

A real friend, in those innocent times, let you cop a "quickie" on top of his bedspread.

And "The Toe" was a real friend. If he wasn't offering his voice, he would offer his sense of humor, an eclectic blend of styles that Whoopi, Redd, Rich, "Moms" and Reynaldo would've been proud to plagiarize.

There were times when he had us laughing at stuff that folks weren't even supposed to even be thinking about laughing about, like cripples and stuff.

Despite the fact that I knew he wasn't reading at the Kissinger-Swaggart level, or a bunch of other levels; I never put where he was supposed to be together, and I guess he wound up suffering from the same kind of indecision.

On a trip back to the "Homeland" (no, not Africa; Chicago, Siberia) we sat up in our overcoats listening to the impotent whistle of a sexy radiator, sipping bad vodka and reviewing the reviews.

He was working as a busboy at the Playboy Club at that time, and lo 'n behold! Hef'n them decided to put on a Celebrity basketball game.

It was going to be like the old days, the "Celebrities vs. the Proletariats." "The Toe," a busboy, was not one of the "Celebrities."

Jim Brown was one, a fair basketballer at Syracuse, and a number of others who would be easily recognizable. But no one knew who "The Toe" was, until he stroked forty two points in. The final score, "Busboys vs. Celebrities" was—Celebrities—30, Busboys—42.

Hugh and folks couldn't really figure it out. How could this pork chop eatin', non-upper-echelon, Black (caps, please y'all) busboy, score that many points against, against, the Best?

That was the real problem; the Best never knew he was the Best, even when he was past his prime.

Chapter 3

Gordon B. . . .

The first thought you gotta think is, gotdamn! This is a big motherfucker!

Big Motherfucker?! Shit! How big was Bussey? Six two, three? 240-50-60-70-80? Yeahhh, he *was* a big motherfucker. And there wasn't a lot of fat on his bigness either, physically or mentally.

I'm always tempted to say that Bussey is one of the most intelligent men I've ever known, not one of the biggest most intelligent but one of the most intelligent period.

We met in the middle of the Army, down in deepest Gawgia; Lawd h'mercy, talk about tryin' times!!

I had fled Chicago to Los Angeles, hoping and praying that the government would forget about me if I got far enough west. It was 1962, chillun.

They followed me with incredibly nasty little memos and

notes—"We want your body." Finally, unable to resist having me, I was lassoed and drug into the induction station.

I keep trying to think of a time in my life that was more miserable. I can't. Even life in the slums, with rats stumbling over your body in the middle of the night and roaches swarming out of your clothes in school wasn't as bad.

There was something so devastating about the reduction of your personality to the level of a serial number that it took me years to get over the shock. And sometimes, even today, I wonder if I have.

The idiocy of the system was exposed to me after eight weeks. The truth of the idiocy sank in solidly when I was sent to Georgia, stood up in a formation of men and realized, after all the names had been called, that my name hadn't been called.

I was a "free" man for two weeks, right there in the belly of the beast. For two whole weeks I stashed my duffle bag somewhere, joined a line leading to some food, ate, slept in deserted barracks at odd times and got in this name brand formation once a day, to listen for my name.

Weirdly, I acquired a girlfriend, too. She was one of the civilians who came on post to make up the officers' beds, work in the cafeterias and do the other slave stuff.

Her name was Ophelia, she was 19 years old, so beautiful she didn't even know it; black like coffee is black and so full of love it was ridiculous.

"What're you doing in here, don't you know this is the officers' quatahs?"

After a week of successfully evading the Army, the enemy, on an Army post, I damn well knew everything.

"How do you know I'm not an officer?" She placed her bucket, mop, broom, dust pan, cleaning cloths and Windex on the floor near the door and began to make the absent officers' beds.

"You ain't no officer 'cause you don't act like one."

She was right. I just sat there, breaking all the rules, watching her muscles dance as she cleaned.

Dear Ophelia, you will read here, for the first time, what I really saw and felt.

By the time she got to wiping out the ashtrays I was desperately in love, desperately. She discovered me hiding out in Major somebody's "quatahs" on Tuesday and by Thursday we had become major league lovers.

I have helped her clean the "quatahs" in ten minutes flat, to give us thirty minutes (her lunch "hour") to make mad love, drunk some of the major's scotch and just lay there, watching mystery winds play with the guazy curtains.

"You crazy, you know that?"

"Why do you say I'm crazy?

"Well, just look what you doing'? You AWOL."

"They don't know that, they haven't called my name yet."

"You AWOL, I don't care what you say. You hidin' out in the officers' quatahs. . . ."

"He doesn't know, he's out there somewhere, terrifyin' the troops."

The nauseous sound of someone calling cadence for a herd of trumping boots echoed through the window.

"And, if all that ain't enough to shake yestiddy, you layin' up in this officer's bed with a woman."

"Not just any woman, Ophelia, with you."

A deathly calm settled the curtains against the window sill as the door knob slowly turned. We felt, for some insane reason, that ducking our heads under the sheets and clinging together would protect us from harm.

"Ooopps, sorry, sir, I. . .uhh. . .I. . .uhh. . .didn't know you were. . .uhhh. .I'll put your piece right here on the chair."

We heard the door close and the footsteps die, our heartbeats bouncing against each other.

A full five minutes later, we cautiously uncovered our heads, to stare at a well cleaned automatic rifle propped across a nearby chair. Some flunky had done his job.

I took advantage of Ophelia's fear paralysis and, after it was all over, she said, once again, pulling up her pink panties, "I tol' you, you crazy."

The next day they called my name, some clerk somewhere had added another card to the file and came up with my name. I was caught.

I dashed back to the officers' "quatahs" as soon as I could, 'bout a week later, and she was gone. Ophelia was gone. No one had ever heard of her. Or seen her.

"Small, about 5'5, stac. . .well built, dark, beautiful white teeth, short hair, full juicy black lips, uhh, uhh. . . ."

"She ain't here no mo."

"Where did she go, I mean, is there a phone number, could you give me her address? I'm her cousin from Detroit."

Nothing. She had officially vanished. I was heartbroken.

BUSSEY: "Don't torture yourself like that, man, it's rough on your peers."

ME: "But, but you don't understand, G.B., she was perfect, she was wonderful, she was divine, she was. . . ."

BUSSEY: "Was she good orally, did she. . . .?"

ME: "She was innocent, G.B., innocent, stuff like that would've seemed like a perversion or something."

We strolled past colonels, majors, captains, lieutenants, not saluting, not giving a fuck about "military courtesy" or any of that shit. I was heartbroken and my new found friend was trying to talk me out of it.

"Don't you men salute officers?"

"Hell—Naw!" We both screamed and ran. How the hell could he find us in the middle of an army post?

We did a lot of that, defiance purely for the sake of defiance. It's a wonder we didn't wind up doing hard time.

But there were other things happening too. There was the town to be dealt with, to be explored. We made preparations for the assault.

G.B. ran back up to his neighborhood (Bed-Sty New Yawk) for a bag of bad smoke over the course of a weekend; like, he and some other dudes jumped in a car on Friday afternoon and got back Sunday night 'round about 4 a.m.

We got ready. The place to go, we had been told, was "The College." We had all heard of "The College" but none of our gang of five hard drinkin', deep smokin', strong lovin' brothers had ever been there.

We floated off the bus, dazzled by the afternoon sun, the humidity, and these finger-sized joints we'd smoked. "The College," "Where?" we croaked, mouths dry as dirt, from the effect of the 'erb.

"College? What college? I been here all my life'n I ain't herd o' no college."

"The college," we repeated.

"Naw, you must a be thankin' 'bout Savannah, they got a college there."

Disgusted with the ignorance of the local population, we ducked into a public toilet to smoke up another j, find the right direction.

"Let's go to the library, they'd know where 'The College' is."

"Right on, blood."

"Oh, you mean Paine College."

"That's what we said."

"No, you said 'The College.' When you say 'The College,' that means the white folks college, everybody 'round here knows that." 1962, remember?

I think we shuddered in unison. I could visualize the grim headlines—"Two drug crazed Negro Soldiers lynched for invading 'The College'."

51

"Uhh, thanks a lot, m'am."

We stiff stepped back out onto Gwinnett Street/Lucy Laney.

The afternoon had folded itself away, the evening was brewing magic, you could smell it as the hint of magnolia, wisteria, mint and corn bread drifted on the air.

"You still wanna trip up there?"

"Hell, why not, she said it was just up the street a ways."

We wandered onto the campus at the right time; the students (serious Baptist institution here, which we didn't know about) had chowed down and seemed to be in a mellow state.

Lovely little campus. To be sure, it might've been smaller than a number of northern high schools, but no place could have been as charming. No place could've given birth to those kinds of trees, that perfume, those beautiful Black queens on scholarship from places like Gimcrack, Musty Toe, Wolfknees, Targum and 'Gusta.

"Look at them, my friend, just look at them, waiting patiently for us to bring them words from the Deep."

To be certain that I looked he placed a ham sized hand at the base of the back of my head and swiveled it around like a puppeteer.

Yeahhh, they sho' nuff did have some fine sisters slinking around. We were like carefully disguised wolves who had wandered into the middle of a herd of innocent sheep.

"Maybe, maybe I'll find Ophelia here."

"If you do, her name will probably be Carmen."

We did that a lot. He called it "intelligentsia shorthand."

We took hold of a position at the base of a giant Spanish moss tree, dripping history and romance.

I think they had a bunch of them in "Gone With the Wind," leading up to the Big House.

"What're we goin' to say to them, G.B.?"

"Don't worry, my anxiety ridden comrade, G.B. will take care of that."

I took a long, serious look at this brother. If it wasn't for the fact that he was so Big, I would've argued with him. Who wouldn't?

Look at him; big, intimidating-looking type person, lazer burn glasses perched on his not too perfect nose, a smile that was permanently eroded by someone's elbow ("a hogan to the upper fronts is what it used to be called"), hardly Errol Flynn in Black. Or in any other colour. But he could draw, I had seen him do it.

A half hour later, 'round about twilight time now, we were being closely attended to by a choice collection of real Southern Belles, Black Belles.

It would be impossible now, to repeat what he said, to pull this academic harem up close to us. I do recall him reciting several pages of T.S. Elliot's "The Waste Land."

There we were, performing a marijuana bravado scenario for two Ophelias, one Carmen, three Magnolia Blossoms and one snappy Nina Simone.

"Where in the world are you guys from? I've nevah heard anythang this outrageous in my whole life."

At one point, I rested my head against the trunk of our stalking tree and listened to the sap flow. It flowed, surprisingly, like G.B.'s rap.

In the twinkling sultry southern twilight, surrounded by the crystalline sound of these virgins, with their faultless minds and dear hearts, I listened to G.B. spool yards of honey off his tongue.

Some of his stories glistened, a few had the texture of velvet and one long, seemingly disoriented tale verged on the Beyond.

As the shadows deepened and two deserters made their profuse apologies—"we got some homework to do"—we gently steered ourselves toward their lips, breasts, arms, legs and the feelings between their legs.

Carmen, the three Magnolia Blossoms and the snappy Nina Simone warmed up to a story that had a pornographic beginning, a sex-lustful middle and solidly lascivious ending. We discovered a reason for exchanging kisses with the five of them.

An unexpected problem prevented us from taking matters beyond kisses. The gang of five wanted to hang together and we wanted to separate them.

A hurried, cross coded conference call between us solved our problem; we'd just deal with all of them together. What difference did it make?

They didn't see it that way. They wanted us to make choices. It's either got to be me or her.

I felt frustrated and angry at the stupidity of being forced to deal with competitive behavior on such a lovely night.

"Look, I have a suggestion," I said meanly; "why don't you five come over to the athletic field with us and race each other around the track. We'll take the winner and the one who comes in last."

G.B. sighed heavily and stared into the distance.

The quintet rose as though pulled by a magic puppeteer and, casting the southern belle version of "up yours, pal!" my way, stomped off into the dorm.

I had blown the whole thing.

G.B. seemed to be asleep for a few minutes and then he clapped a mountainous paw on my shoulder.

"You've got to learn to be more diplomatic, my man, much more diplomatic. We could've had the whole thing, the hens, the eggs, the coop, the chicks, all of it."

"Yeahhh, guess I did mess it all up."

"Well, not completely. I managed to slip a message to the tall one..."

"The one who was sittin' on the right?"

"That one. I told her to meet us back here at 10 p.m."

"When, I mean, how did. . .you?"

"There's a way to do everything, my man, everything."

We wandered off campus to get a pint of rum, something to keep our mota strength at a peak 'til 10.

The tall one, a longer version of Ophelia, snuck around the trunk of the tree with a half filled mason jar of moonshine and a shorter version of herself, promptly at five minutes after ten.

"You guys evah drank white lightenin'?"

"Shit! We was raised on white lightenin'; here, gimme that stuff."

We tippy toed over to their athletic field, a space we had mentally marked off for mightnight fun and games.

The rites were simple and loving. Under the influence of dope, rum, moonshine and, thank God, a moonless night, we played the lover's game in the middle of the football field, somewhere near the fifty yard line.

We did a lot of that kind of thing, G.B. and me, in between all night discussions about whether or not "The Prince" by Machiavelli was still a viable source of political info. Or whether the Kama Sutra was superior to the Ananga Ranga as a text on hedonistic behavior. Or what did "The Meaning of Meaning" really mean.

Some of our barracks mates thought we had made a final turn. And there were others who were certain of it.

"You think those guys are crazy?"

"Do squirrels eat nuts?"

But none of their opinions mattered, we were determined to stay sharp, keep our brains from being sucked into the t.v. or pulverized by the dumbass sergeants latest, most mindless directive.

He was being discharged four months before me. Everybody was discharged before me.

On the night before his return to the Bed-Sty Civilization

we climbed up on the roof of the barracks to smoke a farewell joint.

"This is some of that Panama Red I've been saving for my exit smoke."

The stars were winking at us and the moon flicked benevolent smiles through the woolly clouds.

Panama Red, a sharply raked roof, ebullience.

"Uhh, hey there, my man, I think you better get a grip on yourself, you seem to be sliding off the roof."

I think I was prevented from sliding off the roof by an exercise of Sheer Will.

"Well, I'll be damned. That was pretty good, wanna try it again?"

The next day we shook hands and exchanged farewell pieces of advice.

"Stay out of school, G.B., whatever you do. Don't let Academia corrupt your soul."

"And I say to you, write on, my man, write on."

Steele was one of our companeros down at Fort Gordon, Georgia, and it must be stated, here and now, that he was an unusually hard drinking West Indian brother.

"I'm from St. Thomas, in the Virgeen Islands, mon, and that's where Heaven and God focked. And maybe she came."

Please don't misunderstand, Steele was an extremely religious man, it just seemed that his sense of the Religious was more proundly earthy than that of most people.

"God willin' ah'm gonna wet my spoon in Henrietta's soup tonight."

His sense of the salacious was counterpointed by his alcoholic absorption.

"Steele, we gotta talk about this; I've been told, everything I've ever read, says that alcohol is a depressant."

"A depressant? That's somethin' that make your pee pee

hard, huh, mon?"

"No, no, a depressant is supposed to do the opposite, you know, turn you off."

"Well, mon, ahh I gotta say is this, ah'm glod my pee pee can't read."

It was 1964 (September of the year, to be exact) and Steele was having his unrequested chance to visit Vietnam.

"Why duh fock dey sendin' me dere, I don' know nobody in Veetnam."

It didn't matter. Strangely enough, our brother from the "Virgeen Islands" was a career soldier; he had done 12 years already and had re-upped for three more.

"Now, hey, ah don' wan' nobody to get me wrong, ya understand? Ah luv the Virgeen Islands but ain't a buncha monies to be made, kissin' the tourists asses and divin' f' conk meat."

So, he re-upped and they scheduled him for a short trip to Germany and then a two and a half year stay in "Veetnom".

As an army cook he was looking forward to learning a few "Veetnom" recipes.

"You know somethin', I've ahlways said, we oughta use native foods wherever we go, it would save heaps o' money 'n stuff."

Obviously the bacon and egg guys have never heard him.

In any case, we decided to have a day/night send off party for him. I was designated the "Survivor Specialist" because I didn't drink fifths of scotch and, for some odd reason, I was able to remember the bus schedule departure times.

We started/kicked it into gear at the service club; 'round about twelve noon. I'll never be able to explain how so many of us managed to get off duty at high noon. Maybe it had something to do with the fact that it was on a Friday.

Daiquiris were the biggie. The bartender was a milk shake man to his heart and his daiquiris were creamy perfections.

I lost count after the fifty fifth. By this time we had our own personal waitress and had set a service club record for the consumption of daiquiris within a four hour period.

By the time we slid into the fourth hour, we were onto another record. In the room, the soldiers come and go, never mentioning Michelangelo.

We shifted into second at 4 p.m., when the less privileged got off from work.

Steele's fingers had become Medusa's curls, holding on to his Kool cigarettes.

I slid back in my seat and studied the scene.

A collection of "Lifers"; what they hell was I doing there, a reluctant draftee?

No matter. The military class distinctions had never played a big role in Steele's assessment of any situation.

"Fock it! mon...no matter what it tis, fock it!"

They had been everywhere, shot everybody, killed, raped, pillaged, robbed, supported themselves emotionally by being in uniform.

"Who duh fock cares what's in a fockin' uni-form. We're just fockin' pawns in the big game, ya know whot ah mean, mon?!"

The news that Steele was "pumpin" at the service club spread across the post like waves.

A few officers, incognito to be sure, popped in for a round or two, to wish one of their favorite iconoclasts a safe trip to Vietnam.

"Steele, remember when I had to confine you to quarters for two weeks?"

Unbelievable. It was Major Somebody, I recognized his weatherbeaten face from his class photo. If he could stumble into my life after all this time, then maybe there was still hope for Ophelia.

"Yeahh, major, I remember how ya con-fined me, but do

58

you 'member how I pissed into your salad dressin' ever' day, day in 'n day out?"

"Hahhh hahh hahhah...you didn't!"

"Yes, I surely did."

"You...didn't. Did you?!"

"Elroy, I don't believe you."

The major left a couple rounds later looking slightly green around the eyes. There was no doubt in anybody's mind that Steele had done what he said he had done.

The "pumpin'" and lie-ing went on and on. The afternoon settled into evening, it was time to tackle the town.

We knew we'd have to switch from daiquiris (none of the ghetto bartenders could make them like "Milkshake Mike") and so, a few people added a few security pops for good measure.

We piled into cabs. Some of the ten were already comatose and had to be carried everywhere.

I had never seen anything like this state of Drunkeness. In Chicago, on the Westside even, people got pissed and passed out; I had never seen people get pissed, pass out, come back, get pissed again and pass out again. These were men who were beyond Hangovers.

"I've seen children blown up, women with bayonets stickin' out of their pussies, old people roasted on spits, shit so horrible that I stopped feeling anything about ten years ago. I don't even feel drunk when I'm drunk."

On the town, Augusta, Georgia, 1964, 10 p.m. We had three "night clubs" to polish off; the De Soto, where they had Miles and Monk on the box. The Top Hat, where B.B. King reigned supreme and the Paramount, which was funky boody James Brown/'Retha country.

Steele had no objections to closing any of the joints, his only stipulation was that he would wind up between Henrietta's log jam thighs one more time before he left Georgia.

59

I really couldn't understand it. He and Henrietta were not "lovers." They only seemed to get together for this one event, whenever the urge came down on them.

Oh well, Henrietta for the Finale. . . .

I started noticing a strange thing 'round about midnight, the ten had dwindled to six and at one a.m., three.

The men were deserting, wandering away to their various safe spots, their "shack jobs," their places away from the fort.

We were down to less than three, meaning me 'n him, when he announced, "time to go see Henrietta."

"Gotta remember, Steele, your bus is pulling out at 5 a.m."

"Ah just remembered Henrietta, that's enough."

We had taken the liberty, or rather, someone had had the foresight to check his duffle bag and transfer papers into a locker at the bus station over on Broad Street.

Off to Henrietta's. . . .

It would be hard to imagine a place like Henrietta's now, it was almost unimaginable then.

Steele, as drunk as a human being could ever possibly be, lurched and stumbled in front of me, the point man.

No lights, not even porch lights in this catfish row-alley section of Augusta. The smell of real stale fish and dead garbage were all over the air.

"What the hell is that smell?"

"We're near the garbage dump, the colored garbage dump."

They even segregated the trash back then. I felt like giving up and going back but I didn't know my way back. Back? Back to where?

Finally, after stumbling through a half dozen pools of ditch water (I felt leeches crawling up my leg), we stumbled up onto a porch that looked exactly like eight dozen other rickety porches on the street? in an alley? where the hell were we?

The door opened when we hit the top step.

"C'mon in, I heard y'all comin'."

They fell into each others arms like falling bricks, exchanging some kind of love talk. Sounded like whale grunts to me.

Steele, the Army cook, was, of course, tallish, lean and drunk.

"After ya ben 'round ten thousand poinds o' steak for awhile you lose your appetite."

Henrietta may have also been around ten thousands pounds o' steak in her day too, but she had probably tried to eat five thousand of the pounds.

Big African-American woman; not fat, big. She looked like what a fertility symbol is supposed to look like, all the way down to her beautifully sculptured feet.

Amazing, I thought, to look at this big, gorgeous creature and see these small, delicately shaped feet. Warm lady, full of earth feelings.

"C'mon in, I done fixed y'all a lil' midnight snack. I know this fool done tried to drank hisself to death and ain't had a bite to eat all day."

"A lil' midnight snack" was a soulfood smorgasbord.

The table didn't groan, it creaked from the weight of the greens, beans, salads, ham, chicken, corn bread, pies, cakes; yes, cakes, three, "you know how he like sweets," regional things that no one had ever heard of that didn't live in this section of town.

"Henrietta, where are we?"

"This here section is called the Porto Rican quatah."

"Puerto Rican quarter?"

"Yeahhh, that's what they call it. I don't know why. I live on Chocolate Road."

"Hmmm, this is delicious, what is it?"

"We calls it Porto Rican dressing."

"What's in it?"

"Corn bread 'n lots o' love."

I let it alone and ate.

61

Forty five minutes later, I sprawled back in a junk yard chair and watched Steele and Henrietta make love. The lights were off but my sensitivity to the scene had given me cat-bat vision.

They weren't trying to show off or anything, it was just simply the way it had to be.

The house had a large, all purpose room and a kitchen. The "bathroom" was located in the back yard.

Henrietta had put it to me quite diplomatically.

"I'm gon' give Steele some, do you mind?"

"Well, I don't quite know how to say this but...."

Steele was already stripped down to his shorts.

"Well, you can go sit in the kitchen. Or you can go outside. It's kinda chilly now...or...."

"Fock that, Henrietta! He's a grown up! Turn off the lights 'n bring it on over 'ere!"

The lights went off and she joined him on the sofa pull out bed. I relaxed in my chair with a plate of "Porto Rican dressing," which seemed to taste even better in the dark, and during one especially rhythmic period, I ate a big piece of sweet potato pie.

Deep experience. After an hour of watching these silouhettes do this incredible ballet in bed, I began to dream about Ophelia.

Henrietta brought me back to the real world with a tap on the foot.

"Steele 'sleep. You want some too?"

I couldn't figure out what to say, what to do. Did I want some?

"Uhh, why don't I take a raincheck?"

"Ain't no rainchecks for Henrietta baby."

We let a full, pregnant minute ooze between us, before she said, "Well, don't say I didn't make you an offer."

At four fifteen I was staggering out of the "Porto Rican"

section; Henrietta's directions to the bus station clicking against my brain, Steele draped around my neck, "Porto Rican" dressing, a couple chicken breasts, half a cake and a pocketful of corn bread weighing me down.

We made it on time, retrieved his belongings from the locker and, as he mounted the bus, turned to me and said, with extreme lucidity coating each word, "Thank you, my friend, thank you. Tell Henrietta that I love her, O.K.?"

The bus station was in the white section of town and when I left it, the sun was coming up and the local cracker cop was strolling down the street, his hand on his pistol.

"Hey boy, whatchew dewin' ovah heah in this port o' town this early in the mornin'?"

"Non' o' yo' fockin' bizness, motherfocker!"

I'll always think the Spirit of Steele closed my body off from the six bullets that the racist fired into my back. Ase.

Chapter 4

My return from the "Wah," as someone once called it, took me back to United States Post Office at Canal and Van Buren ("for sick leave, call WA2-9200") and back onto the world of the Felt'.

The world of the Felt was lined with silk, rimmed with expensive fur and surrounded by beautiful women.

Interesting brother, infinitely interesting. I used to stand off to the side and watch him after my return, to try to get a handle on him, his action.

He had done the Army thing too, but for him it was an apartment in a classy section of Paris. I was sent to Georgia. There is no need to make contrasts in order to dramatize what always seemed to be happening with, or to him.

Who in the hell ever got drafted for duty in Paris? I wasn't the only one who marvelled at that.

It seems that I've always knows B.F.; maybe it has something to do with growing up in a place like Chicago, where familiar strangers wind up getting married. Or becoming friends. Or enemies.

When we were younger men, going to different high schools (Dunbar and DuSable), he was a familiar stranger. Later on, we became buddies. I think we became friends during the course of my second marriage.

Those were the days (or rather, nights) when we left the post office with a select couple ladies for an evening of logic and/or love. Or maybe a trio or a quartet.

We have to start with women, if we're going to take an objective look at B.F.'s world.

We hung out together at one crucial point in time, meaning we psychoanalyzed ourselves and a varied selection of incredibly interesting women. Those were the nights we spent tripping around the North, South and Westsides (we saved the lakefront for special events), spreading joy and hope.

It was definitely inspiring to many, the level we took what was commonly called "The Rap" to. We never allowed the scene to deteriorate to a mere chat for cunt.

In the dimly lit bars and noisy dance halls of the Bantustans, we dazzled the multitudes with our own fierce logic and disguised lusts.

We sat in the four poster booths, tryst-sipping cognac, gazing into the chocolate flavored eyes of Nubian queens, snow-whispering decisive points to Fulani sisters, Ewe fantasy-dolls, Tunisian rockettes, Congolese JuJu women, Azanian Amazonics.

B.F. didn't work at developing harems, or struggle to surround himself with ladies, they just always seemed to be there.

He had, at one period, six of the most beautiful Black women in the Chicago Post Office. I remember discussing the situation with a jealous, would be rival, one afternoon, over a couple before-going-to-work gin 'n tonics.

Would-Be-Rival: I can't figure it out, man, I really can't figure it out. The motherfucker ain't handsome worth a shit, he definitely ain't good lookin' as I am."

"I'd say he was rugged, you know, manly lookin'."

"Fuck what you say. I say he ain't handsome."

"Well, hey, what's handsome?"

"He don't dress in no spectacular way, not like me."

"He seems to be well dressed whenever I see him."

"Aww man, you know what I mean?!"

"You talkin' about the difference between being an exhibitionist and having good taste."

"What's that mean?"

"Skip it man, let's punch in."

Yes, six of the most beautiful Black women in the Chicago Post Office. And three in the wings.

There was S., who was perfectly shaped, beautifully dressed and lovely to be around.

There was the "Yellow Woman," the large boned, lush creature with the full lips, wide hips and breasts that invited you to touch them. Her look was a challenge to any man who loved women. B.F. used to make her wait for him.

The other four were of various shades, dimensions, attitudes and they were all intelligent. He couldn't stand to be around airheads and fluffbrains.

(For reasons of diplomacy, everything written from this point on has to be considered strictly confidential and in the *past*).

He would pick a choice, tender, intelligent woman out of the crowd, pull her toward the heat of his mind and turn her out, well toasted.

No male chauvinism here, just the truth. I was privileged on a few occasions to be there, to listen to it happen.

The woman is fine. No doubt in anybody's mind about that. She has been told that she is beautiful so often that she is almost bored by the compliment.

She has not had anybody praise her mental beauty, or disabuse her of certain false notions. One of them is/was that she was the most desirable piece of goodness that ever had thighs.

We tripped off to the intimate little bar on Cottage Grove, the one owned by the lil' ol' grandma who made the best daiquiris in the world (yes, even better than "milkshake Mike") and had never tasted one because she didn't drink.

The music may have been Donald Byrd's ("Cristo Redentor" or " 'Round About Midnight." Miles and "My Funny Valentine" were definitely on the box).

My lady and I gazed at each other in the dim light, flickering sex holograms on each other's minds as we listened to B.F. and Miss Fine twist their tongues around inside each other's heads.

B.F.: "Who told you that I wanted to go to bed with you? Who led you to believe that?"

Miss Fine: "Well, isn't that what this is all about? The soft lights, the drinks...this is delicious, incidentally; your bedroom tone of voice..."

B.F.: "I'm beginning to get a slant on the kind of dudes who've been pursuing you. You've been taken on a lil' stereotyped romantic merry go 'round. I want you to scratch my name off that list."

Miss Fine: "I wasn't saying that you were one of them, I was saying..."

B.F.: "You were saying that a man who speaks in a well modulated tone of voice, who knows where the pleasant surroundings and excellent drinks are, can only be after one thing.

"Would it surprise you to know that I come here by myself sometimes?"

Miss Fine: "I'm sure you do, but you've got to admit that

you do have an ulterior motive for bringing me here, don't you? Could I have another daiquiri? They're really delicious."

B.F.: "Just raise your hand, she'll do you again. Ulterior motive? Yeahhh, I got an ulterior motive.

My ulterior motive was to be out with you for an evening, to determine if you were the sort of woman I could trust, that I could be friends with, that I could exchange points of view with, that I could talk about what was happening in the world with, far away places and doing exotic things."

Miss Fine: "O woww, all that?!"

B.F.; "You want me to stop there?!"

Miss Fine: "Is there anything more?"

B.F.: "It all depends on you."

And so the evening went, fueled by daiquiris and mellow vibes.

We did that a lot. And the funny thing is that the brother was good as his word. There are at least six Miss Fines tripping around at this very moment who are graduates of the School.

But that wasn't all, the ladies. There was the philosophical section that would sometimes immerse whole taverns in what was happening. And it wasn't the "Is God Still Alive" kind of stuff.

He'd quietly get down to the grit without seeming to change stride, taking a few diehards, kickin' 'n screamin', along with him.

"Hey, let's face it, by this point in time in our racial history a lot of Black people, African-Americans, are in a bad way because they don't know any better.

"Look at it this way; it's like a trained animal, a dog, maybe, who was chained to a tree by three yards of chain and when the chain was let out to six yards, he was still circling the three yard perimeter. For some of us, maybe most of us, the chain perimeter was rejected in the very beginning. Can you dig where I'm comin' from?"

Midnight 'til dawn seemed to be the best of the B.F. times.

He loved the perfumes of the evening, the electric emotions, the nuances, the shadows, gestures and postures.

"Felt, what do you make of that?"

The Apartment, downstairs, a Southside-summer time, a little past the bewitching hour.

He'd focus on the situation over the rim of his upturned wine glass.

"Hmmmm. . . middle aged man with Sugar Daddy tendencies, out with a chick who's probably going through her virgin act for the third time this week."

He was inevitably correct in his appraisal of the situation, which seemed to spare him the problems of weaving himself into situations that he couldn't immediately unravel.

"She was going to be a problem, I had to cut her loose."

"I mean, but how did you know?"

"I could see it."

He had the foresight to put a portfolio together while a lot of us were still thinking about the bi-weekly paycheck.

Coldblooded brother.

"Would you actually shoot to kill."

"That's what .45s are designed for."

"But, you know, would you actually shoot to kill?"

"If I fired on a motherfucker, it would be to kill, not to maim. A maimed motherfucker could come back to you; a dead one, never."

In some circles, already, what he is about is almost legendary.

WOULD BE RIVAL: "I don't see it, man; I've never been able to understand it."

OBJECTIVE BYSTANDER: "Understand what?"

WOULD BE RIVAL: "Well, I've never been able to understand how this motherfucker be doin' the shit he be doin'. . ."

70

O.B.: "Like what, f' instance?"

W.B.R.: "Yeah, o.k., well, anyway, we all there, the music is pulsatin' and everybody is feelin' pretty mellow, if you can dig where I'm comin' from?"

O.B.: "I get the picture."

W.B.R.: "In pops the 'Great Lawd Felt,' from somewhere. The rumor was that he had just tripped back from another trip to the Coast. Or Brazil, or somewhere."

O.B.: ""I'm pretty certain it was Brazil."

W.B.R.: "Well, o.k., Brazil. Anyway, there was this sister up in there, 'bout 5'9 or 10, black as a piece of coal and so fine that two or three of the brothers had offered to pawn their pinkies to try to get off into her panties. The sister was a star, you hear what I'm sayin', the sister was a Star!"

O.B.: "I heard you brother! Release my arm!"

W.B.R.: "Oh, sorry 'bout that. I just couldn't help get a lil' excited. I mean, 'cause she was a sho' nuff stomped to the bone star. I'm talking about the type of sister that sends dudes away talking to theyselves 'n what not.

"I had waited 'til "Fast" Frank Fiddler rapped and faded in the stretch. I knew I had "Donald the Mouth" beat by a length because, well, by the time he got through tongue rimmin' his lips 'n shit, that was all there was to that.

"'Donald the Mouth' is the brother whose career in high school basketball was ruined when somebody elbowed him in the mouth. Quiet as it's kept, it fucked his sex life up too, but that's another whole story."

O.B.: "Ahhem! You were talkin' about the Star?"

W.B.R.: "The star?! Oh, yeahhh, we was all shootin' at the star. I was just about to edge up on her and throw my lightenin' bolts at her head, just as he came in . . ."

O.B.: "The Felt?"

W.B.R.: "Yeahhh, him. I don't know what the mother-fucker said to the broad, but a half hour later she was following him out of the door. I was so pissed off, I couldn't resist askin', hey, what's he got that I ain't got? You know what this bitch said to me?"

O.B.: "This what? You know we're into ourselves now, brother; we don't say nigger, bitch 'n a few other things. . ."

W.B.R.: "Yeahhh, I heard that. You sound like him. Anyway, you know what she said when I asked her what's he got that I ain't got? You know what this b. . .you know what this sister says to me? She tilts her chin up in the air and says, 'He's got charisma, that's what he has that y'all don't have.'"

O.B.: "Charisma?"

W.B.R.: "Yeahhh, that's what she said; what's charisma?"

O.B.: "I think it's like being rich; if you have to know how much it costs, you can't afford it."

I understand what the sister, the star meant, in addition to something else; the Felt understands what Friendship means, and that goes 'way beyond charisma. We checked it out one night in #206.

Chapter 5

Marshall always made me think of a Tutsi King. Or some
other royal African figure. Maybe it had something to do with
him being 6'9 or 6'10 (when he straightened up completely).

Elegant Black man, that was the agreed on picture that we
all shared. It wasn't a foppish elegance, something that could
be attained by wrapping a certain number of a certain kind
of clothes on your body, no, his came from somewhere else.

When we played around in junior college for awhile, and
took showers after gym class he was elegant in the nude. It
was in a gesture, a posture, the unique expressions that lin-
gered on his face. Natural elegance. 6'9 or 10, lean as a whip-
pet and when last seen, couldn't play basketball worth shit.

I don't really think the game held that much interest for
him. Or maybe he didn't care for the sweaty part of it.

In any case, it was always funny to see people start drool-
ing when they picked sides for the ever lasting, on going

basketball games that kept the Southside jumping and pumpin' all summer (fall and, with little snow, winter too).

"We got the tall dude."

He was graceful as a ballerina, until he got his hands on the ball. Something seemed to happen that no one could predict. He might pass the ball to the other side, or simply dribble it out of bounds. Or do something equally strange.

No one could figure it out. Here we got this real tall man who gets outpositioned for a rebound by a 5'8 inch pygmy.

I can never recall anybody laughing at his actions, there was nothing to laugh at because he wasn't funny. He was puzzling. Sometimes some of the stuff he'd be doing was so puzzling that he'd score points because the opposition had fallen away in confusion.

Like I said, I don't really think the game held that much fascination for him.

He was fascinated by other things: clothes and Spanish sherries, for example.

When I stated earlier that his elegance wasn't dependent on clothes alone, that's the truth, but his sense of style wasn't an obstacle to his elegance either.

6'9, dark chocolate, classical Africoid face. He wears a closely checked English hunting cap (in the summer, snow white), an old school tie (real ol' school), a hand woven Phillipine cotton shirt, beige velvet vest, a houndstooth sport jacket, grey French slacks and a pair of handmade Italian loafers.

Sometimes, in the fall, before the chill of winter made all of us ashy, he'd wear leather gloves.

"I hate for my hands to get cold."

"Who taught you about clothes, you know, how to put stuff together?"

"My old man was a gambler, a big time gambler, who followed the marks across the United States to all the big places. Except 'Vegas; he thought 'Vegas was a tasteless place to go and make money.

"His thing was Hot Springs, Arkansas, Saratoga, New Orleans, the Kentucky Derby, those classy spas where you had to have money or class to be on the set.

"He didn't have a lot of money, not in comparison to the people he was gambling with, but he did have class. Pounds of it."

That's what Marshall had, class. He demonstrated it to the max, on at least one romantic occasion.

Her name was Bernie and both of us had fallen in love with her. How could you not fall in love with Bernie?

Bernie was an African-Cherokee princess who spoke as though her voice was piercing chocolate veils, and the tones traveled through yards of wisteria before it reached your ears.

I had a Lithuanian racist, the most virulent kind, an immigrant, say to me one day in the Wilson Junior College basement—"I be Black, I love Bernie."

We bes Black and we did love Bernie. Bernie was totally seductive. She had a dancer's body, 5'5 and slow as blackstrap molasses. Every rhythm she had was slow, except when she danced.

I couldn't believe it.

One evening we (Marshall and myself) watched her do a six-eight pelvic movement for forty-five minutes; it was unreal. Was this the beautiful Afro-Indian sister we watched drift around the Wilson Junior College campus every day? The mistress of slow motion?

The die was cast. If either of us had had doubts before about what we wanted to do with her before the six-eight exhibition, it was all dispelled; we were deep into the rut, bull deer fever had infected us.

Interestingly enough, it was Springtime. . . .

We took to riding out to see her in Altgeld Gardens (a

suburban Soweto of Chicago).

We'd pretend to be there to bring her the latest news about what the deal was in the literature class, or try to cross examine each other about the meaning of farting in the Sulu straits. Anything.

One evening, in the middle of our verbal pyrotechnics, she stretched out on the family sofa and slept for a half an hour. We patiently waited for her to return to the world of the witty before continuing.

We had no choice but to sit there and watch her.

If there was such a thing as a sleeping vestal virgin, she was It for that evening. We sighed whenever she took a deep breath. Or fluttered an eyelid. And when she snored, gently, to be sure, we slid back in our seats and imagined her feathery curls in the crooks of our arms.

After a few months of this we were beginning to feel a bit ragged with each other.

What was happening?

One morning, sipping our first surreptitious cups of apple wine in the campus shoppe, he looked down at me (even when we sat down, he still had 10 inches on me) and said, "Look, let's deal with this sensibly. You dig Bernie and I dig Bernie too. And it seems that she digs you more than she digs me. So. . . ."

She digs me more? I didn't know how to function with that one. It seems that we had become such an entity, the two of us, that it would've been impossible to imagine one without the other.

We haggled for a bit. I didn't feel secure enough to say to him—"Look, man, she digs us both. Can't you see it?"

I was honest enough to say to him, "Look, man, she doesn't seem to really dig either one of us all that much. If she did, why the hell would she go to sleep whenever we visit her?"

"Awww, that's just defensive mechanism bullshit. Either

that or she's just tired as hell."

Whatsoever. We gradually faded out of the scene as another dude cleared the air that we had been cluttering up.

While we were still trying to decide who was going to be Mr. Bernie, the brother slipped right in between us and ripped the sister off.

"Guess what?! I have something to tell y'all. I'm in love. I'm really in love, me—Bernie from Altgeld Gardens."

We cried on each other's shoulders; with difficulty, but we did.

The romantic focus of our existence gone, we retreated to the grape, sherry to be exact.

Marshall's sherry drinking, like his talent for wearing Italian hats, was a deeply cultivated taste.

"Awright now, check the color of this Palomino out. See how golden it is. Get a little whiff of the bouquet. Now taste it. You get that creamy nut taste? Now, here, do the same with this Fino. It's real dry. . . ."

We didn't spit out tastes into a container, or do any of that madness. We sampled and drank every drop.

Many evenings, probing the secret corners of English literature, we'd "sample" a couple bottles of Director's Bin, or a Shooting Sherry or two.

It's a safe bet to make that we slithered through the whole Bristol family of sherries; the tawny, the Milk, and wound up in Jerez de la Frontera.

The sherry drinking was, in a sense, our response to the pressure of Junior College. We were simply marking time in Junior College, waiting for something to happen.

The English lit class ("O young Lochivar is come out of the West. . .") would have been completely wasted without the graceful taste of the sherries to ease it along.

We also shared another kind of reality, the Post Office. It happened a few years later, after we had stopped marking time at the local junior college, written Bernie off as a mockery of the romantic impulse and got down to the stupid business of being non-affluent African-American citizens.

One evening the brother strides over to me, he was wearing a dark silk shirt, white cotton pants and a pair of two toned loafers. He was, as the expression goes, as clean as the Board of Health.

He seemed uncharacteristically distressed.

"Dig, man, you gettin' ready to go to lunch, huh?"

"Yeahhh, guess I'll get out there and have a quick glass of sherry."

"Would you do me a favor while you're outside?"

"Yeah, what?"

"Find me a length of pipe or iron and check it into the checkstand."

"Sounds like something serious going on."

"I got this motherfucker fuckin' with me in my section and we gon' have a little 'session' when we get off. He's a big sonbitch and I don't want to be wrestling with him and get my clothes dirty. Besides I wanna lay somethin' upside this stupid asshole's head that he'll remember for a long time."

"You got it."

I was fortunate to be able to trot right across the street from the post office and find a section of "designer" pipe for my friend.

It was about the length and width of a broom stick. Nice grip to it.

The guard at the lobby checkstand didn't even blink when I checked it in and got my receipt-ticket. Someone put out the rumor that a farmer had tried to check a goat one time. Just a rumor.

"Here you go, man."

"What's it look like?"

"Nice piece of pipe, it oughta do the job pretty well."

78

"Thanks, brotherman."

The following afternoon I read with real interest the story of a post office "altercation." One of the parties had been hospitalized with a fractured skull.

I closed the paper, took a sip of my Duff Gordon 28 and smiled. There was nothing like the satisfaction of helping a friend solve a problem.

Fred wasn't quite as tall as Marshall, but without any exaggeration it's safe to say that his Ego made him at least 10'10.

Another classically featured Africoid face, but not from the west coast, this one was from the northeast, Egypt maybe. Or Ethiopia. An Aristocratic African, from wherever on the continent.

A six footer, his body held so straight it seemed that he was being held erect at the shoulders by some invisible force, one that had had an effect on him alone.

When I first met him he was well on his way to becoming a controversial legend, that is, some people liked him intensely and some people disliked him with equal intensity.

But, I'm getting ahead of myself. Let's go to the beginning.

The Post Office/1958-61. Richard Wright had just stopped working there. Well, it had been twenty years past but there were old timers who could tell you what they talked about.

Sterling Stuckey, the historian writer, worked there. Plus an incredible collection of linguists (one man had memorized the grammatical structures of four Romance languages but couldn't speak any of them), encyclopaedists (one man had read the whole set of Brittanica), crazies, artists, mathmeticians, astrologists, aliens, drug addicts, transvestites, nuclear physicists, low and high grade morons, freaks of all persuasions, escapees from other states, every thing.

The 8th floor, at the peak of the work day (6:00 p.m.), harbored every kind of human being this earth has ever known, emotionally, at any rate.

Fred and I started talking. Conversation was a cleverly developed art on the 8th floor, at 6:00 p.m.

It had to be a cleverly developed art, if you wanted to be heard above the thunderous murmur of 2,500 people, the clash-bang of hundreds of machines, the general throb of mail factory.

We hit it off right away, for some unfathomable reason. We seemed to have almost nothing in common.

He was going to the University of Chicago and I had flip flopped out of Junior College. He was into opera, the classical European composers, fine foods and divine wines.

I didn't understand Opera, had never paid much attention to anything classical and hamburgers were a treat. I did know a bit about sherries (thanks to the tall one) but nothing to brag about.

But we hit it off. We took those unauthorized breaks together that the p.o. jargon labeled "pots," and he made an effort to talk to me about "Descartes' Meditations."

I'd never heard of anybody named Descartes, let alone his Meditations. Fred threw a coat hanger at my head and left me in the lockerroom, puzzled.

Why in the hell would anybody get pissed off about a dead Frenchman's book?

A couple years later I understood a little better and, strangely enough, books were being thrown at my head, not coat hangers.

In some convoluted fashion we had become tenants in the same building, on the same side of the fourth floor.

I can only think about the building we called "The Avon" in the most affectionate way.

The "Avon," or "the Avon Towers," for the satirical, was one of those rare, free form universities that the beaurocracy, the government or whoever holds the Stick, will automatically tear down, wherever they find it.

This sturdy four storey brick on the corner of 61st and Dorchester bristled with intelligence, information, music, geopolitical understanding, the stuff that television steals from human beings.

We had all the stuff there and it was reinforced by the hour. Fred lived in 404 and I lived in 400. We were just close enough to get on each other's nerves and just far enough to stay out of each other's hair.

I have to admit, at this late date, I must've been a glorious pain in the ass.

It seemed to me that I suddenly had an intellectual plus dropped within reach and I was going for it.

I felt he was fleeing his guruship if he didn't answer the four hundred questions I had for him every day.

The man had read everything. And seemed to have the kind of sophisticated approach to life that I wanted to develop.

When we gathered in each other's rooms on Sunday evenings to drink cheap red wine and dissect the political structures of the world, I'd find myself amazed to watch him remain silent as some would be know it all ran his mouth off.

"Fred, you know what that guy was saying is a bunch of shit. Why didn't you call him on it?"

"Why should I? To give myself the satisfaction of knowing that I had put a fool in his place. I don't need that."

It took me a few more years to understand how heavy silence can be.

Fred gave parties in his room, some of them became Events, sets that some of us can recall because it was the first time fifty people had done the samba in a space that was only slightly larger than the average toilet.

In some ways "the Avon" was the perfect setting for a Fred. On Sunday afternoons, when he closed his door for an all day session with the Brahms 2nd, or Sibelious, or Berg, no

81

one thought it was strange. Peculiar, yes, but not strange.

He had a style that made him unique to his friends. Whether he was marching through the streets, obviously listening to a drummer that none of us ever heard, or glaring at some poor goof who had made the mistake of crossing him, he was unique.

And he will always be.

Chapter 6

Ralph is unique too, but not in the same way that Fred is. There are times when I've wondered if "Ralph" wasn't an imposter, and that the real Ralph isn't hiding around the corner.

I have seen, over the years, so many facets of Ralph that it would be totally impossible to take a sharp look at any one face of Ralph.

Those of us who've known him over the years could compare notes and I seriously doubt whether we'd come up with a definite picture of the man.

"Ralph? A MARINE?! Be serious. Ralph, a Marine, back in the days when Marines was really Marines?" That kind of Marine? I couldn't imagine any such thing in my wildest dreams.

"That would be like trying to picture Odie as a submarine captain. He really and truly was a real Marine?!"

That would be one Ralph to some people.

One could also easily get the picture of another Ralph, a flashy type who dressed like a "two hundred missions" man, complete with black silk scarf whispering in the wind, as he piloted his "el" train to the next stop.

"47th Street! 47th Street! Transfer point for east and west surface lines. Watch your step as you exit the car, please!"

What we've been looking at is someone who has been able to make adjustments, acclimate, re-orient themselves in positions and to situations that most people never attempt to get into. One example comin' right up. . . .

"Well, I must say, Mr. Vernonnn; unusual spelling of your name isn't it?"

"I don't think so."

"Ahhem! Well, what I mean is that most people named Vernon usually spell their names with only one N."

"I got bored with only one N."

"I see. Now then, let's take a look at your application. Hmmmmm. . . I'll say this much, we don't often get applications to fly our planes from people as well qualified as yourself."

"I'm glad that you're pleased."

"Uhhh, Mr. Vernonnn, we seem to have one slight problem, discrepancy, you might say. Right here on line 15, where it requests that you put down the number of hours you've flown and the type of craft. You have 6 hours in a Piper Cub, . . .don't you mean 6,000 hours in a Piper Cub."

"No, it was 6 hours in a Piper Cub."

"But, Mr. Vernonnn, you're applying for a job as a pilot for Pan Am, we fly the biggest planes in the world around the globe."

"I understand that. Are you aware that a man and woman flew around the world in a plane without an engine?"

"Yes, I'm aware. But that's another story, Mr. Vernonnn.

They weren't carrying 200 people to Singapore. You do understand what I'm saying."

"Of course."

"I'm terribly sorry that we can't bring you aboard, but your lack of experience, well...you understand...."

"Certainly."

"Maybe if you went for a few more hundred hours in a larger craft."

"What's your engineering department look like, any openings there?"

"Oh, you've had engineering experience?"

"One could call it that, if one wanted to."

Don't attempt to adjust the picture, it's coming in this way because that's the way he is.

Personally I like to feel that Ralph and I have come closest to sharing a private view of the Theatre of the Absurd than almost anyone I can think of.

But first, for dynamic categorizing, let's break the brother down into those three basic eras that a broad scope of his activities seem to suggest.

There was the Old Ralph era, which gave the germ for the Middle Ralph era, which is certainly responsible for the New Ralph...era.

The Old Ralph era was a feverish period, for Ralph and the people who went in and out of his sphere of influence. During the Old Ralph era he was considered the most dependably undependable person anyone had ever known.

He could pledge a death ritual—solemn agreement with you one day and forget about it completely, until the next time he saw you.

His way of pulling this business off became so intriguing that an adjective was credited to his name.

"To do a Ralph" meant that you had sworn a solemn oath and splashed the sacred blood of the Honey Booger on your forehead and then promptly forgot about the whole thing.

When asked the question, "What happened to you?"

The answer was apt to be, "Oh, I Ralphed."

For those people who set Ralph up as a Guru, during the Old Ralph era, and "Ralphed in, Ralphed on and Ralphed out." Well, some of them are still "Ralphing."

During Ralph's "Ralph" period, during the Old Ralph era, you'd need an odd sense of humor to deal with him.

We're returning to the Theatre of the Absurd that I spoke of earlier. To begin with, he was always open and agreeable to do anything, go anywhere.

"Hey, man, you know what we oughta do, we oughta hitch-hike up to San Francisco and hang out for a few days."

"Sounds like a winner to me. You're kinda tight with that lesbian broad you met at the Festival last year, when you went with Palmer and the gang. What's her name?"

"Judith."

"When do you wanna leave?"

"How 'bout this evenin'."

"You're on!"

I cannot remember the month, but it was real cold hitchhiking up 101. Real cold. Must've been November of the year.

It was a beautiful trip. Ralph, the old ex-marine, (yes, he did know the legend of Chesty Puller) one of the few who could be satirical about it, walked beside me in the dark.

It was ink black in places, stars floating in clusters over our heads, moonshine dancing off of huge boulders that gleamed like alien creatures.

We counterbalanced. He felt I was badly in need of a shrink to propose this, and I felt he was equally spaced to accompany the idea.

A succession of the sweetest people in the history of hitch-hiking drove us straight on into San Francisco.

The last driver on our journey, a crazed member of the

last regiment, deposited us in the heart of the Fillmore District.

Ralph, the Hedonist, is suddenly glorying in the idea of being in a place where unbridled sin is always on the track.

"Look it that! Them is genuwine, authentic—live 'hoes!''

We finally made it to Judith's Powell Street apartment, after wading through hundreds of yards of perfumed sin.

The ladies had marked their territory five yards apart, using perfume, leather coats and sequined smiles.

"Let's walk back through here, this is the kind of shit I like to see in America."

The brother had never seen San Francisco, but he became a San Franciscan after the first hour.

Yes, Judith was this top flight lesbian sister I had met at the Festival and, of course, we were invited to stay in her apartment.

Ralph went beserk, in a sophisticated way. The brother has never been prone to uncool shit, even during his Old Ralph era.

He was caught up by and with, everything. Above all, as a dyed in the ghetto Middlewesterner, he was tripped out by the bodaciousness of these Western bulldaggers.

"Heyyy, lookatthat, they're feelin' each others' titties, shouldn't we be doin' that?"

"Uhh, not necessarily, not here anyway."

We cast about the city like trout fishermen. We shared baroque conversations with people getting on the bus with burning candles in their hands. The bus driver patiently holds one of the candles whilst his incandescent passenger digs down through her various layers of rags to pull out the fare.

Ralph, an ex-public transportation expert, thinks aloud, "I might still be doing my number if I had been a bus driver in 'Frisco."

One afternoon, going somewhere-nowhere, the four of us,

Judith, Ralph, Pat and myself, got involved in a serious chat with a transcendentalistic metaphysician. This can only happen in San Francisco.

Our lesbian friends, jaded, de-bussed, leaving us in the shimmering wake of the metaphysician.

We were so enraptured we got off the bus with the Transcendentalist and walked a few blocks with her, trying to figure out how anyone could be so stacked and talk so much crazy shit at the same time, real off-brand shit.

Oddly, two things happened simultaneously; the transcendentalist metaphysician disappeared and it started raining fiercely, metaphysically.

We were suddenly lost, (well, not really, but we were on unfamiliar ground) broke and baffled by the transcendentalist's disappearance.

What to do?

We held a two man powwow and decided to walk the streets calling Judith's name, hoping she'd hear us and call back.

I'll never be able to figure out what Primeval Thing this gave off for us, but it supplied us with a totally wonderful hour.

There we were, trooping through the rain, under the guise of calling for somebody selling something called "Judith!"

We had rationalized ourselves into an opportunity to stroll through the streets of a modern metropolis, screaming out loud.

We became Operatic after a bit, going from screams to arias. . . .

"Ohhh Juuuuuddddiiiithhhh! Ohhh Juddd. . ." Well you get the picture.

I can't remember if she heard us or not, but somehow we found our way back to her apartment, screaming and wet.

Spontaneous dude, the Old Ralph. Every moment was spent lavishly. We must've "bankrupted" ourselves on two or three occasions, emotionally.

Judith and her lesbian harem, conservatives, thought we were degenerates, just for the way we talked. And the things we were doing.

One evening, walking somewhere, we decided to let ourselves be picked up by a couple Gay brothers. (A word of caution before preceeding. We had presented brutally effective heterosexual credentials to the world for so long that we both felt jaded by the effort. Dig where it's comin' from?)

Judith, Queen of Lesbos, caught hell from her community for what followed, but that's another story.

We were in San Francisco, we had read Jean Genet; shit, we knew what sailors were and what they did on leave. We were drunk enough to think that we might be charming enough to cozy up to a lil' cognac, a good Cuban cigar, an hors d'ourve or two. What the hell!

"Let's go for it, you game?"

"Why not?"

Good Old Ralph. . . .

We wound up in this gorgeous building overlooking the Bay, beautifully decorated, lush plush.

We were having a perfectly fine international time until this weird smelling dope began to circulate.

I thought it was PCP and jacked myself up into a fake coma. Ralph, quick to sense that we had arrived at the end of the 3rd act sooner than expected, played me off into his paramedical bag, complete with thumbs in the eyeballs and pulses.

"Damn, he's having another one of those attacks!" They hustled us right on out of this gorgeous apartment overlooking the Bay. Who in the fuck wants somebody throwing fits in a swank suite overlooking the Bay?

After we had been vengefully deposited in a sleazy all night greasy spoon, we called Judith to come pick us up.

In a few profane moments we were made to understand that

we had played on a couple good friends of hers. She was highly pissed.

But, above and beyond "incidents," I think they grew to enjoy us. Ralph went militarily Bohemian, took to wearing a red neckerchief as a sign of his whatever it was.

He could have been in a west coast Pamplona. Or maybe on Mykonos, in its yeahhh day.

Since that trip he has, of course, rebelled in many other ways.

Each of his "rebellions" (the Middle Era) has explored a new facet of his personality. Or this society's personality.

During the Middle Era, he got off heavily into hypnosis, but never seemed to be able to hypnotize anyone that I can think of.

Palmer had a brew during his session and closed it off with a malicious Marine Corps smile.

None of it seemed to bother Ralph a lot. "Don't worry," he said, "you'll regret that you were not hypnotizable some day."

We blinked and went about our business.

It was obvious that he was changing. In the Old Ralph era, we would've been relegated to the anteroom and forced to read Time magazine.

The New Ralph is almost devastating. The New Ralph utilizes the wild moments of the craziest years, to discipline Anglo-Saxon technocreeps, to explore the most esoteric of the esoterica....

"So, you want to create a memory for your Berimbau, huh? Well, that takes patience."

The New Ralph has placed the Old Ralph into the proper perspective, and only uses any of that when it is properly necessary.

The New Ralph takes cues from the news of the day, the feeling of the moment and dances only when the music is right.

The New Ralph offers warm vibes, gives generous emotional gifts and intelligent decisions. But one is constantly reminded that a split decision can trigger yet another facet of Ralph. "Whose next?"

I've always seen Palmer in Technicolor. And sometimes in 3-D, without special glasses. Maybe it has something to do with his image as a kind of Superbrother; strong, intelligent, driven to live each moment as though it were going to be his last.

"Let's hit it!"

'Mitch 'n the Night Trippers,' friends of his who've driven and been driven to the far corners of the country because he loves to go.

"Let's hit it!"

We drove all over southeastern California one day, drinking beer and pontificating, something we'd never think of doing these days, the beer drinking part, that is.

Mystical dude, in his way, in his love for the "Inside," Nature.

Strange, sometimes, to know someone from childhood to manhood, to watch them suffer the slings and arrows of outrageous fortune, to watch them grow.

Palmer, the offensive blocker ("if you got enough nerve to follow this trail of blood and broken bones I'm gonna leave you can score a t.d."), the defensive terror—"send both of 'em over here, I got two arms and two legs!" Palmer, the man inside the boy.

The Marines' (he and Ralph, the "Old Ralph," together in New Zealand, wandering through exotic time zones) and onto the Sparklett's water wagon.

The water factory never had a better salesman. He probably would have been able to pour tap water into those five gallon containers and sell it just as easily.

But the water wagon is not where the brother's story begins or ends. His story begins in relatively simple machisimo and scales upward, into serious sensitivity.

For years he has walked and rode on trails that only the Indians know about. When you watch someone out in the middle of where human beings *are* supposed to be, behave as though he belonged there, you feel something slightly holy about that situation if you have a spiritual bone in your body.

He acquired a brute force rep by doing what He-men used to do; flattening bodies out on the football field, and the basketball court too, if you were foolish enough to believe he was actually going for the ball. The huntin' 'n fishin', the hard livin'. But there was always this Other Side.

It's possible to obtain a uniquely different perspective on Life by being in the company of a person with a rifle on his shoulder, who knows what it's for, who merges with a sunset. Or wakes up before everyone else in order to brew a fresh pot and watch the Earth revive.

He is one of the few Black men with Indian ancestors who is, I think, more Indian in his feelings about the land than anyone I know.

Palmer stories form the repetoire of quite a few folk singers. Right here are two of mine; we are going somewhere. You're always going somewhere with him, if you're within a hundred yards of his motions.

Me and him and our two ladies, he's driving us through Angeles National Forest with the most perfectly mixed quart container of high brow gin with a whisper of vermouth and a spout to let it out.

No one in his right mind would do it now, but at one point in the wild 'n woolly past, circling high cliffs and plunging into subterranean valleys was always fueled by alcohol.

It was almost the custom.

All four of us were in what might be termed "a state of g-ace."

We drove in slow motion past Forest Rangers and toasted them at 4-6 thousand feet. We paused at lookout points that had no signs, no designations stating that this was a lookout point.

We tilted forty five degrees forward and didn't fall into the abyss. I don't know why.

We snuggled the car up onto a trail that trickled off to the right and the left. We eased out of the ride and onto the trail and found our way to the Red Man's trysting places.

Me and my lady made love on a thorny hillside, facing downwards, braced by holding onto a couple cactus plants. We must've looked like a couple of yeti in a "Wild, Wild World of Animals" sneak preview.

"Wowww! Look at that!"

We clinched ourselves together, the sun glazing my naked ass, the gravelly slope scraping hers, studying the coldbodied movements of four ruby throated hummingbirds.

It was only a chance climax that alerted us to the fact that we were sliding into the Abyss.

"Let's hit it!"

Weeks later we tried to hit the moon. No joke, we set out to do it and no one is certain whether we succeeded or failed.

I think it was Ralph's idea.

"You know, I think we oughta shoot the moon tonight, the forecast is for a full one."

Palmer immediately agreed, "Sounds like just the thing to do."

I was given a WWI Mauser to clean and within an hour became a willing convert to the belief that it could be done.

Ralph reassured us that it could be done if we found the right hill and allowed the proper trajectory to work. He also got off heavily into his own brand of astrophysics, which seemed to make a lot of sense, to him.

Palmer took things to another level.

"Hey, the hell with all that lip music, if we say we gon' shoot the moon, let's shoot."

He knew just the spot, a hill, a small mountain actually, near La Mirada.

We drove to the rendevous, checking and re-checking our weapons.

Someone had asked, just before we hit the road, "Where you dudes going?"

"To La Mirada, to shoot the moon."

I can still see the look this person gave us, a friend, to be sure, but not a believer.

"Going to shoot the moon, huh? Well, bring me a little piece back."

We smirked at his sarcasm and wheeled away. We parked the vehicle on the shoulder of the road and started up the side of this mountain, quietly, cautiously, never once taking our eyes off the prey.

It could've been Everest because by the time we got to the peak I felt as though we had walked up through three time zones.

Extremely quiet night, clear. We hunkered down, as though we were listening to something. Or for something. Waiting for the right moment.

Palmer suddenly brought his piece to his shoulder with one smooth motion and said one word, "Now!"

We trained our sights on the moon and, in the kneeling position, blasted away. Ralph told me later that he had tried for an eye shot. Palmer went for the heart. I was praying to hit the fat part.

We stood after the last bullet fell into orbit, sweating from the passion of the moment.

"What do you think?" I asked rhetorically.

"We got it," they chorused and started running down the mountain; leaping and jumping along behind them, I felt like Ali following Lawrence of Arabia into battle against the Turkish hospital caravan.

The following week I happened to be in the neighborhood (I'd be lying if I said I wasn't searching for a couple moon chips) and I started up the side of the mountain, shaking my head in disbelief as I stared at the gopher craters, the tangled roots, the shallow wall of cottonwood trees clutching the soil midway up the mountain.

Trees? I doublechecked the place on the map. Yes, I was in the right place, on the right mountain, there were even spent shells at the peak. Trees? How could we have run down this horribly scarred hillside without running into the trees? "Palmer, do you know there were trees on that mountain we ran down a couple weeks ago?"

"Damn right, you mean you didn't notice?"

I think I caught the glimmer of a twinkle in the brother's eye as he redirected his attention to a cool one.

But it wouldn't've mattered in any case, if the trees had been there or not. If he had decided to run down the hill he would've ran, and he would either have run over the trees or they would've moved off to one side to let him through, recognizing one of their own kind.

Chapter 7

If I've seen Palmer in technicolor and Ralph as a man of many faces, then George fits into his niche as a Moralist. I think Brother G. was the first member of our peer group who actually said, "You shouldn't do that, man, it's wrong."

Unreal. Ethical Behavior 101. And he's always been like that. Always.

I'm pretty certain that I first became aware of this abnormality in him when Herb and I described our encounter with the nymphomaniac in the basement.

"So," he says, looking at us with Odd Couple contempt, "so, you chased these little dudes away and went in there and attacked that poor little girl. I don't know what to say about you two, I really don't."

"George," Herb tried to plead, "she wasn't a poor little girl. She had a nice little turd cutter on her and she wanted to give us some stank. Simple as that."

"But it had to be pretty obvious that she had a mental problem."

"Who in the hell thinks about mental problems when you trying to get your pee pee wet?"

He stayed disgusted with us for a couple weeks. In his eyes we were morally degenerate and no amount of joking could pull him out of it. "George, what should we do, go give the pussy back?"

Herb used to say that he became the way he is because he grew up on Washington Park Court, a relatively pleasant, somewhat middle of the class street a few blocks south of 47th Street.

There may be just a grain of truth to that, but it still doesn't explain where his sexual morality came from, and that's mostly what we're concerned about here.

When we were at the stage and age of allowing our hormones to govern our sexual urges, George was in Another Place.

"George, look, man, I know she digs you."

"How do you know?"

"Well, 'cause she told me. Herb heard her, didn't you, Herb?"

"Clear as a bell."

This was a very nice girl I'm talking about here, very nice. Her name was Joyce and she sho' nuff had the hots for Big G.

Herb and I had a vested interest in playing matchmakers, we were doing it for the delicious snacks involved.

Here's what the Real Deal was: Joyce's mother was one of these avant garde types who believed that she should know her daughter's friends, male and female, be friendly with them, fix snacks for them.

Snacks, that's where we were. It seems purely mercenary to think about now, that we should've been trying to put our friend's arms around this gorgeous young lady so that we could trip over for snacks.

I think the quality and quantity of the "snacks" added a bit of spice to the push. Ham on rye, pickles, potato salad, potato chips, hamburgers with everything you wanted to put on them. Coca colas by the case. "Snacks."

And the chance to watch the Game on a large screen t.v.; we had found Paradise. All we had to do is convince the reluctant lover.

"Uhh, George, you goin' over to Joyce's later on?"

"I hadn't planned to, why?"

"Oh, no reason. . .we were just wonderin', you know."

"George, I got an idea! Why don't we trip by Joyce's house?!"

"For what?"

"For what? To say hi to her mom, have a snack."

"Damn! That's all you dudes think about."

We would usually get our way, because we were his friends and he has a generous heart. However, there were times when no amount of coercion would work.

We even tried to use Joyce's charms to obtain a permanent place at the snack counter.

"Joyce, I bet you a dime you won't kiss George on the lips and gently allow your tongue tip to probe the inside of his. . . ."

"Betcha I will!"

"Betcha you won't!"

"Hold still, man, and let this girl kiss you so I can lose my dime."

"I can't believe you dudes, you all will do anything, I swear. Anything."

Joyce, finally tiring of the effort to win dimes, married somebody we'd never heard of. Herb and I were grief-stricken for weeks, the snack bar was closed.

It wasn't that George didn't like girls or that he didn't attract them. He did like them and they were attracted to him like moths to a flame.

We could never figure it out. Tallish, slender guy, hatchet faced, slue footed, with his knees shooting out in different directions. Someone made the observation that he had been one of DuSable High School's slickest faking quarterbacks because he had hands like catcher's mitts and an eggbeater way of running that confused the defense.

In any case, from the earliest times, the ladies beat a path to his door.

"What is it, tell me, what do you see in the brother?"

"It's. . .it's his eyes, they're so, so. . .so dreamy." George's eyes dreamy? They usually looked bloodshot to me.

"So tell me, what is it, what do you see in the brother?"

"It's not what you see in him, it's the way he makes you feel."

"George? The way he makes you feel?"

"You want to hold him in your arms, you want to protect him, mother him. . . ."

And on it went. Beyond his "dreamy" eyes and the maternal instincts he seemed to provoke, there was, incredibly, his dancing ability.

I have to say incredible because his normal way of moving, kind of a shuffle, gave no clue to the spectacular turns and dips he would uncork, once he had been persuaded to "git down."

Herb swears that while they were stationed in Germany he used to attract a circle of admirers whenever he shot out onto the floor. I believe it.

I didn't see him on the dance floor in Deutschland but I caught his act lots of times at parties in Chicago.

In Chicago, attending Wilson Junior College (with tall Marshall) the brothers morality play continued. I'm not going to lie, I was as poor as a poor person can be, trying to go to school.

There would be days when the rumbling of my empty gut would turn English literature into an endurance act.

Under the circumstances I felt no hesitation about picking up food whenever I found it. And it was fairly easy because most of the students were well fed and careless with their brown lunch bags.

The school had an extraordinary number of Eastern Europeans (Hungarians, Lithuanians, Estonians, Poles, Russian Jews) and they made their sandwiches with wonderful rye bread.

"Hey, man I wanna talk to you."

It never took more than a couple minutes to wolf their large sandwiches down, leaving me feeling prepared to deal with My Conscience.

"I saw what you did."

"What did I do?"

"You stole somebody's lunch."

"Burp! Stole?! That's a hard word, brotherman."

"Oh yeah, what word would you use?"

"I'd say I found somebody's lunch and it became mine because I found it."

"What kind of logic is that?"

"I don't know but it justifies filling up my belly."

Generous soul, he took to bringing jelly and egg sandwiches to school. He'd carefully place them where I couldn't miss seeing them and then bitterly complain about forgetting where he left his lunch. Or else he'd quiz me, knowing that I would lie, naturally.

"You see my jelly egg sandwich? Man...I left it on the top shelf."

"Uhh, naww, naw. When did you put it there?"

"This mornin', when we got to school."

"Somebody probably stole it."

"Yeahhh, I wonder who?"

The food thing didn't really get to him that badly; it was, once again, the sex thang that broke his code out into open.

In a fierce whisper in front of the locker. "Don't you have any scruples? Can't you see that woman is blind?"

Yes, of course, I could see that Regina was blind, blonde, stacked like a brick shit house and had a dog named Tinka. In addition, she was pulling down better grades than either one of us.

"What am I doing that's wrong? All we do is talk and sometimes have a cup of coffee."

"Who buys?"

"Well, she does usually, she has the money."

We wound up having a round table discussion about the matter in the Music room, the fantastic studio on the third floor of his family's home, where we went to listen to "Bird" and cool out.

Herb was my ally.

"You know what this dude is doin' at school, he's messin' 'round with a blind woman."

"George, blind women need a little pee pee every now 'n then too."

It didn't matter that we hadn't reached the pee pee stage yet, me and Regina. What mattered is that Herb had planted a seed in my skull. Nothing ever developed from it but, like I said, the seed was planted.

Junior College slipped away, the Army experience behind, a collection of us drifted westward to the American Riviera, California.

George's experiences on the European continent seemed to have blurred his clear cut moral judgments somewhat. Or, at least, made him a bit more tolerant of mere mortals.

"Wait a minute, let me get this straight. You mean to tell me that you're going with that woman *and* her sister?"

"They said it was cool with them. Why not?"

"Well, do what you want to do but you know what they say. . . .?"

"What's that, brother G?"

"God don't love ugly."

I stared at his back as he bent over to pull one of his famous spinach pies out of the oven, puzzled to the brim.

God don't love ugly? The Du Barry twins, ugly?

Only George's God would think such a thing.

Chapter 8

Dean's epitaph might read: "The brother who tried to fail and almost succeeded."

I don't think you meet Deans, I think they spin in on you. I could tell that there was something circumnavigational about him, the first evening we stopped off for a drink at the old Parisian Room, right after our weekly writing class.

A personality that contained a sneeky leer and a really dirty laugh and the ability to scream "ugggghhhh!" and a few other quirky things cued me into where he was comin' from.

I didn't know he was an alcoholic until years later, not even after I had watched him throw a tantrum in the parking lot of a liquor store.

"I just gotta have a beer, I just gotta! I just gotta!"

Up 'til that very moment I thought, well, the brother is a heavy drinker, an alcohol abuser, just like most of the artists I knew.

It was kind of strange about the alcoholic thing, it seemed to form a fringe element for what his problem was about, but an essential fringe, without it he was too sober to be around.

I used to ponder that, heavily. You mean to say that we have someone here who is a better person drunk than he is sober?

It seemed to be that way, except for the fact that he was always changing. I could place Dean, like Ralph, into three distinct categories; like Ralph, the "Old" Dean would do anything imaginable.

He was, at one point, the tenured staff person of a middle league California college, responsible for giving Stokely Carmichael and H. Rap Brown a chance to air their grievances. Imagine that....

It is to be said that his old period was shapely, designed to fit the stereotypical picture of a young Black man on the way up. Why it went another way is anybody's guess, but while it was happening, it was as they say, awesome.

Dean, as a writer, will always hold cards for me, it was his personality that seemed to get in the way of what was supposed to be happening.

We *must* mention his supportive woman right in through here.

Despite the fact that most white people *never* think of African-American women being *non*-supportive, a bunch of the pop Black literatures have decided to support the stilted view of the Black woman as minor league shrew, who was so programmed to keep her drawers up and her dress down, that she would never righteously support a struggling brother's artistic efforts.

Dean's wife kicked all of that in the ass. As a ghetto raised San Bernadino sister, she knew what hard times were all about and, despite her intimate knowledge, was willing to back her man to the hilt.

She *did* back her man to the hilt. "You want to write, baby? O.K., go 'head, do it to the max. I have an excellent, well paying easy job that I like, I'll earn the money, I'll supply us with the day to day stuff, all you have to do is write. O.K.?"

Sister was so fine, both inside and out. She purchased a house for this fool. He was furnished the downstairs for his personal writing needs and the rest of the house for his bullshit. I couldn't believe it.

From time to time, in response to his invitations I would trip up to San Bernadino for an afternoon of cheese chippin', hors 'd'oerving and heavy talk.

"What's the deal with you, brotherman? You got a dynomite lady here, the best environment any writer could possibly ask for and yet you seem to be trying to find out where you can buy a chunk of failure. What the deal is?"

"C'mon with me, let's go to the bank."

I went to the bank with him a few times, to draw out his wife's money, to buttress his fits of silliness. After a few times I couldn't go anymore.

I'm sure I didn't come off like George, the Moralist, but somehow I couldn't make myself believe that a brother was pissing on a golden opportunity.

And that is exactly what he was doing. The dude in charge of Black Exposure on a pre-dominantly Anglo campus quietly became a disturbance of everybody's peace.

"I don't know how long I'm going to be able to put up with his crap. . . ."

We'd wind up at parties where he'd be sure to piss in the hostess' pet flower pot, the avocado she had raised from a small core. He'd alienate anyone who could be alienated. He described his procedure as "searching for the underbelly of it."

As a Howard U (or was it Morgan State?) grad, he had a

lot of underbelly to search for. He practically envied my atrociously correct slum background. "You've already been under the underbelly, you're jaded."

It wouldn't register in his bright brain that poverty can't be romanticized about, hard times are hard on everybody.

"Yeahhh, that's what I gotta do, I gotta get to the underbelly."

If he had searched for a success as a writer with the same intensity that he shot for the underbelly he would've been a Black Hemingway in 6 months.

"C'mon, man, let's trip over to the Red Velvet Turtle."

"What's that?"

"You'll see."

The Red Velvet Turtle was old hat for me. The Red Velvet Turtle was the 430 Club without sawdust on the floor, Pitts Pub, without the "Brutality Booth" where the gorilla pimps used to go and slug their women in the chops.

The Red Velvet Turtle was filled with tension and hostility.

"See that motherfucker over there? He put that other motherfucker's eye out last year. Walked in here and shoved a rifle barrel into his eye."

After 8½ minutes I'd be bored shitless in the Turtle. And semi-scared because you could never tell when and where the tensions would spill over. Dean was intrigued by all this cruel shit.

"This shit excites me."

"What's there to be excited by?"

"The undercurrents, the unreasonableness of it."

"Oh."

He could always find an answer for it, it was the people around him who couldn't find the answer.

"But why, Dean? Why?"

"Why? Why? Why? Why? Why? Why? Why?"

"Fuck it!"

The kinks became a bit much for some of us, and the sarcasm that was fueled by the alcohol. It was as though he expected you to appreciate his shit.

His lady stuck it out for a very long time and finally drove away in her Peugeot. "I can't take any more."

A number of his friends decided they didn't need friends like him. It was a bit like watching someone disintegrate.

It became quite obvious that he had found the underbelly. He was laying on it. The collegiate ladies in his life slowly became one-eyed gunny sacks with wine bottles stuck in their purses.

"What're you trying to prove, man?"

"Nothing, I'm not trying to prove anything. I dig Gluedy Mae."

"A forty six year old woman with five kids, on welfare? What's the future with her?"

"Who knows? Maybe we'll have a kid, settle down somewhere, drink ourselves to death."

It was always weird to find out what his latest thing was. He discovered jail.

"Peace and greetings from the Inside. . . ."

"Dean? In jail? For what?"

"Burglary, believe it or not."

"Peace and greetings again, from the Inside. . . ."

"He's back in again?"

"Yeah, same thing."

We exchanged letters like shotgun pellets for awhile, 'til his insensitivity caused me to hang up the pen. He had become an asshole behind bars.

After another short bit he returned to the scene, unrehabilitated, older.

"What's gonna happen to you, Dean?"

"What's gonna happen is already happening."

It's a little like watching someone back up in the fast lane at 5:00 p.m.

There was a time when I thought self destructive people were drawn to me because of something in me.

Fortunately, a very hip buddy cooled me out; "Don't look at it like that, brotherman. Self destructive people are drawn to everybody. That's what makes them motherfuckers so destructive."

How did I come to know J.C.? Maybe, I guess, in the way it's been done thru the ages, through his converts.

He could've been Benny, the hazel-eyed realist who, at ten years old, challenged us to jump off of this second floor scaffold into a mountain of soft sand and buried himself head first.

When we finally got adult aid he had already been dead for fifteen minutes. I saw my name being screamed out between his clenched teeth when they dug him out.

He could've been Eli, the Dope Dealer, who was busted (after successfully peddling large sums of Bolivian cocaine) for six "overweight" traffic citations.

He could've been a whole bunch of guys I've known who were practically punch drunk from the ability to beat themselves. But he wasn't any of those, he was Something Else.

J.C. was always there, had always been there. He was Miles' "Kind of Blue" before Miles knew he was blowing the blues. As a matter of pure fact, J.C. gave many people their first taste of what the blues could be like.

But, we're getting ahead of "ourself" (as J.C. would say, semantically pissin' around).

After a few months of hanging out with him, I knew that it was useless to try to deal with him as a regulation personality. After a few months, I realized that I was dealing with too many minds inside too many heads, and some of them were dangerous.

My fondest hope is that the brother will laugh, or at least smile when he reads this. I will have to be careful from this point forward, but caution has never offered any guarantees with J.C.

I will praise the blues singers; he was a super blues aficionado and critic, a rare species in any society, who understood what "Howlin' Wolf," Muddy, Leadbelly, Lightenin', B.B., Lou and Joe were talkin' about.

I met him at Mz. Martin's place, that genius of people swapping. He was semi-hostile to me at first, but it was only because he had had a bad day, one of thousands.

So, there he is, there we is. He grin-smiles and doesn't trust me worth a fuck and I know he is really an undesirable alien, but with eminently righteous qualifications.

He is an honest mechanic in Southern California. Shall we cock our legs up higher and plunge deeper?

J.C. was a mechanical genius, one of those modern men for whom the car and the horse were built.

"Did it cum yet?"

How can you explain this fantastic mechanic (circa 1989) who is also in the upper places of Drama?

How did I get to know J.C.? Well, like I said, he was always there.

Yes, he was always there but he had never tried ouzo.

"J.C., I've had enough of this Canadian Club. How 'bout some ouzo?"

"What's that?"

"Ouzo is a Greek liqueur. You can't drink it, you gotta sip it. Wanna give it a try?"

"Why not?"

Simply put, that invitation jacked up the sale of ouzo in the non-Greek areas by 150 percent. Now we have an 80 proof, anise flavored liqueur mounted by a man who loves to race cars and bet on race horses.

He drinks the ouzo by the fifth and goes to the race track to taunt the innocent and play prince of bettors with the horses.

"J.C., how much have you ever won at one time, betting?"

"That's not the point, whether you win or lose, it's being there that matters."

The brother is extremely sensitive and constantly on the lookout for insults of any kind. Strange experience to be somewhere with someone who knows how to make real logic happen and kill it off with a completely contradictory action.

The layers add themselves; ouzo, horses, cars, insecurities.

"I'm gonna kill that son of a bitch."

"For what? Why?"

"Well, uhhh, there's got to be a reason."

The Actor. That was one of the more surprising revelations. The scene was written for someone who could bring a taste of madness to the set, the Moment is then. . . .

Small hairs on the back of our necks stiffened out, watching him play the jaded, doped out owner of a nightclub, after all of the patrons have left for the night, including Justine, the lyrically shaped, Ethiopian looking cocainist.

His laugh was manic, his actions were bizarre (he actually masturbated) and his level of drama took us to another plane.

He could also do cheap acting too, those moments when he wanted you to believe that everyone was wrong but him. Everyone was *always* wrong but him.

I sometimes felt the gambler had woven a net for the actor to fall into.

"Damn! You believe this?! I got eight warrants for my arrest."

"For what?"

"Mostly tickets."

"Why didn't you pay them?"

"Why should I?"

"Because they arrest you for stuff like that."

"I was playing percentages. Guess I lost."

Periodically a comination of personalities welled up in his skull and leaked. I took careful note, they were usually Womanizer-Fool-Neurotic Artist. Leaks.

The womanizing section was mostly mental and took the crudest shape possible.

"Look at that ass! Hey! No, not you! Your friend! You wanna lift somewhere?!"

"J.C., must you holler out of the car window like that?"

"Awww c'mon, man, don't be such a stuffed shirt."

The Fool usually surfaced after he had sank his face into the uozo cup too deeply, too often. The Fool was almost medieval. He wanted to have adult women play "Spin the Bottle" or "Pin the Tail on the Donkey." Or do more absurd things than that.

The Neurotic Artist was filled with facets from the other two forces and, I suspect, more "legitimate" than they were.

He was a Neurotic Artist, almost a magician when it came to dealing with cars, but "out to lunch" on the people level.

A complicated example of what I'm talking about follows.

J.C., for a fee, is willing to take the Iyalosha Tanina Songobumni around to the used car lots. He knows which cars are lame in the left rear hock, which ones have been injected with Speed 'em up for the days inspection. He knows cars but has not the slightest idea of what an Iyalosha is. Or does. And really doesn't give a shhit.

It didn't pose a problem for the Iyalosha, she could laugh her way thru anything. She almost laughed her way thru four years of cancer. In addition to everything else she understood J.C.'s Ogun.

"Man, do you know what this woman did?!"

"I have no idea, tell me."

"We need to get a bottle of uozo before I can bring myself to talk about this."

He had forty two carefully chosen pitstops around the city. He could pull up on a deserted corner, dart into a building behind a building and pop out with a bottle of uozo. J.C., the Magician.

"O.K., so there we are in this lot. We've looked over everything in the place and I'm ready to cut it loose.

"The situation basically boils down to a choice, between this yellow car and this blue Volvo. I'm not really excited about either one, but if I had my druthers it would be the yellow Datsun 310.

"O.K., I'm standing there, trying to work the salesman's head a little bit when I notice that Tanina has disappeared. No problem, I think, maybe she went to take a crap or somethin', you know what I mean?"

"I read you loud 'n clear."

"God, I love this stuff. Anyway, ten minutes go by and we're like ready to close the deal. No Tanina. I excuse myself as though I have to take a trip to the shitter, to tell her, 'c'mon, baby, I think we've struck a pretty good deal for the Datsun'."

"Mind if I have a sip of that?"

"Ohh, sorry 'bout that. I'm walking through the yard toward the shitter and I happen to peek off to my left, between some cars and there is this woman down on her knees, playing dice with some coconut shells. I couldn't fuckin' believe it!"

"Couldn't believe what?"

"I couldn't believe that number one, a grown woman would be playing on the ground with some fuckin' coconut shells. And especially not now. We were there to buy a car, not play games.

"I didn't say anything and I didn't let her know that I had caught her acting nutty."

"J.C., J.C.?!"

"Lemme finish, I know what you're gonna say. She's a godperson or something, right?"

114

"An Iyalosha of Shango."

"Eyeyah byyah! We went to buy a car. We get back to the salesman and she announces that she has decided to purchase the blue car, the Volvo. I couldn't fuckin' believe it. And she did."

"How did it work out?"

"I don't really understand it, that piece o' shit wasn't supposed to make it out of the yard."

"And it's still running?"

"When I last saw it, it was runnin' pretty good. Say, man, what's the deal with those shells?"

"Why don't you ask the Iyalosha?"

"She's dead, remember?"

"Why should that prevent you from asking her questions?"

Ahhhh, but there was always more to J.C. than the sum total of these small parts. This is the brother who has driven miles off his track to help a stranded customer, the ruthless gambler who would invest his daily double winnings on a settling sunset.

A strangely fragile dude, despite his macho stances, a man who would appear in a rainstorm with a wrench and a good heart, an honest mechanic with integrity. How much more could you expect from any man?

Chapter 9

I always ran when I was with Leonard, maybe it had something to do with the fact that he was a natural 440 man and I had the dashes covered up to the century.

Leonard, Jake "the Fake" and I spent one glorious summer stealing, ripping off. It started off being a fun thing and became a vicious fever.

In Chicago, on the "El" platforms of the Southside, we snatched wristwatches from commuters' wrists as the train pulled out.

We went to sporting events (track meets, basketball games, baseball games) and with well rehearsed diversions, raided the unsophisticated cash registers of the day. We were so fast and so smooth we were unreachable.

A single coded glance would be enough to spur us into synchronized action. The door of the delivery truck is open, the milkman is delivering. Let's do it.

The summer was over, fall rains had made gutted ruts out of the alley I dashed through. The milkman, a youngish Black dude is on my trail. I refuse to drop the tray of milk for the first fifty yards but my man is gaining on me, I must drop it.

I shot out of the alley next to 48th Street station just as they were changing shifts. I will never forget the curious looks I got from the city's finest.

The milkman was a beautiful brother, he had to be because all it would've taken was one yell from him, "thief" and they would shoot the shit out of me.

In those days, "Two Gun Pete," one of the most sadistic of the "finest" used to blow people away for talking back to him.

The milkman retrieved his milk and me and Leonard hooked up at the Stickhall later on, to drink a lil' Irish Rose.

"You know something, man, I was just thinking. I think it's time for us to retire."

"You know something, man. . . I agree."

The three of us divided the hundreds (even we were surprised!) of watches, rings, necklaces, money we had snatched and ran with. And went straight.

Years later, when Leonard and I lived on different floors of "the Avon," we would sit around on a Sunday afternoon, listening to Monk, "Pres" and "Lady" and reminisce about the summer we stole.

"Seems like a dream now, doesn't it?"

"It was a dream, otherwise we'd be doin' time right now."

We turn West for a moment or two before heading East again.

Terry could definitely relate to what we did, to the summer we got away and he got caught.

But hold on here, how can we get to Terry without going through Troy?

Maybe some people love suffering. I wouldn't include Troy in that category. He never gave me the impression that he loved suffering, but I received the impression that he was suffering, spiritually, anyway.

We were custodians together. Being custodians could've meant that we were pariahs or people who felt miserable about ourselves, lower on the caste scale than security guards. None of that kind of feeling was happening in either of us. Nope, none of that stuff.

Like I said, he may have had a smidgeon of the spiritual blahs going on, but no internalized ill will.

So far as we were concerned we were the creme de la creme of this fucked up society and the work we were doing kept our brains free to do our own work.

My mind offers me three avenues to Troy. The approach to one of them has us mopping and waxing a football field sized floor in some County office building, sincerely discussing the latest bullshit that the government has dished up to us. Or Afrikan-American networking. Or whatever.

Troy, like the manager of his apartment building, Terry, was someone you could talk about anything with.

Kind of a Wild Thinker, psychologically, able to twist and glide anywhere, for whatever reason he designed. Sometimes he did it for the sheer intellectual fun of it.

Extremely logical, but a bit crazed at times; it always had to be a bit more complicated for Troy.

We tripped from Thales to Sartre and from Socrates to Shakespeare and back and forth across the floors, swinging our industrial mops like vindictive swabbies.

There was always something essentially intellectual about Troy that supported his eccentricities and, at our last reunion, I found that still to be the case.

We often slipped (while mopping) from philosophical infantilismo (I mean, after all, what the hell did we really care about what the Europeans thought. Or think?) to sophomoric reviews of other cultures.

"Onion eating, garlic eating cultures are doomed for extinction."

"You mean for 'stink-tion'."

You could do that sort of number with the brother. However, somehow, he managed to erect a barricade around himself without closing himself in. And that's the way he's been for the past ten years. . . .

Terry, who was Troy's apartment complex manager when I first met him, has always made me think of him as the original hipster, the kind of dude who could go dead to sleep in the middle of the fastest action around and still be ahead of the scene after he woke up.

An original man of nuances, flavorings, shades; he looks hip, acts hip, bes hip, is hip. How did he get to that state? Well, in some ways he was always there, lodged in that pantheon of hipsters (R.B., Elijah, BoBo, Billy Woods, Johnny Fox, Herb, Armando, Ralph, Ron, Palmer, the Du Sable graduating class of June '56) who were too cool.

Some of them were so cool that they froze up, became dead men and didn't even know it.

Terry flirted heavily with the cool death for a while, he talked about it.

"Yeahhh, baby, that heroin, y'unnerstand what I mean, that heroin was on me, it was me. *I* was heroin for the time I used.

"I was *too* cool.

"While I was cool I had a gin-u-wine monster on my back that was colder than I'd ever be. The monster weighed a long ton and I was bent. God only knows how I managed to buck him off, to free myself of the outrageous beast!"

His language is quintessentially linked to a frame of reference that gives murderers and the murdered names, faces, families, fingerprints.

A many faceted dude; sometimes, when the mood comes down on him, he'll redecorate his whole house, plant beautiful women in the backyard, paint a miniature masterpiece, give a large warm party.

His laughter, during these times, borders on the tenor saxophone level, gets musical. I've stood off to the side and observed, when he was too heavy and when he trimmed down to his hippest weight, and each of those states seemed to carry their own elements, swim in their own juices.

I was appointed Godfather to his son, a very hip move indeed, and allowed the priviledge of seeing the hip father at work.

"Heyyy, you can go on 'n do that if you want to, baby. . .understand what I mean? But that's not something I'd do if I were you, the price will be too high in the long run. You unnerstand what I mean?"

Portions of his style were rained into his drinking water, sifted into his bar-be-que, released in his skull after the lockdown. Or whipped upside his face as he tricked through the fleeting memories of crooked streets.

"Was it wrong, y'unnerstand what I mean, to do the dirt I did? Damn right it was wrong but I felt I had to do it. That's what grabs a lot of these young dudes. It's like a contagious disease."

Over the years I've watched the scenes change, the acts revolve, listened to the language (both sacred and profane) danced the good dance while the baaaad music played, enjoyed the brothers hip.

Some slithery headed type once asked, while Terry was in the middle of what he does best, "How old is that dude?"

The answer came from a body to my left, "How long has jazz been our music?"

That's how hip he is. . . .

I was hired to teach a writing class at the Watts Towers Arts Center in Watts, under the creative directorship of John Outterbridge, on the basis of a two hour soul rap.

It was so deep I told Terry about it.

Beautiful human being, the 'Bridge, clean, in charge of himself, creative to the bone, loquacious, sincerely interested in the welfare of people.

I don't clearly remember what we talked about, but evidently it was good enough to have me on the scene for three years, sometimes with only one student in the class.

The 'Bridge has been the Director of the Watts Towers Arts Center for ten years or so and has done so much for the artistic community that he should be considered a national treasure.

Those of us who know him well are always saying to each other that we have never heard a negative word about John Outterbridge.

There are probably no bad words to be said about the 'Bridge. And that's saying a helluva lot.

Creatively, the line has to stretch from the 'Bridge to Henrique and Cedric, and it couldn't go anywhere else.

Cedric and I had talked about Capoeira, after having seen, heard or been subliminally introduced to the art via Black Belt magazine and the rare Brazilian film that utilized a piece of it.

The short form; Capoeira, an African-Brazilian martial art that was developed in Brazil by African escapees from Portuguese enslavement.

Cedric literally discovered our teacher (I was on a Tae Kwon Do hangover at the time) in the forests of upper Echo Park. A real complex situation developed immediately; three of the most complicated people in Los Angeles get together for Capoeira lessons. The fourth complicated person, the instructor's wife, deserves a book of her own. Maybe two books.

It took me a month to begin to see Henrique, the Teacher, and Cedric, the Student, as younger brothers.

It wasn't a distant, patronizing look, not the look of a blood older brother, but the look that the seasoned perspective living long enough is apt to grant any man who is using his muscles seriously. And his mind consciously.

Henrique was a marvelous teacher, patient, gifted with philosophical insight about his art. It was fairly easy to see that it would be possible to play Capoeira with anyone, after having received his instructions.

We created a roda, the three of us, and I found out a few things about two people that I probably would never have known under ordinary circumstances.

To learn Capoeira, for an African transplanted anywhere, has to be the equivalent of a spiritual experience. I saw it happen to Cedric.

During subtle afternoons, the sun settling sideways and the birds chirping in the trees around us, Cedric's eyes glittered like diamonds. It was Capoeira.

Henrique, the stylist, held himself in reserve so that you never really knew how much he had left, in a manner of speaking. I could sometimes see him as a species of berimbau (when I wasn't playing with him), a slender stick of wood, a creature of many moods, delicately structured but tough and resilient.

He introduced us to independent rhythms, those effervescent sentinels that take hold of the soul's juices and allow you to experience dream-play, the times that make you ask, hours later, "What did I do?"

He was at ease with himself and I saw that as a great statement, philosophical and otherwise.

It was an announcement that we could play together, harmonize our motions and yet remain individuals. The Afrikan

123

in us was being given carte blanche.

"Play your own game, but feel what I'm doing."

The brother's art was to the bone. He wasn't, isn't Pastinha, Gato, Rizidinha or Bimba. He was—is—himself.

I think the bloom-example of his sense of aesthetics flew out at us a year after the last lesson. He began to make kites.

Yes, of course, we know everybody makes kites and the Brazilians make some of the best kites of all, but these were more than that, these were kites that took us for rides. . .uhh huhhh. . . .

He was constantly surprising. We knew Cedric was an artist, someone who could take an ordinary number-two soft-lead pencil and create infinite things, black super images. . . .

Henrique took our sensibilities to what could be done with ink, black paint and ivory white paper. His midnight scene of people on a deserted beach doing the "frevo" is haunting.

As we continued to play the Capoeira game across the hillside faces of Los Angeles, from Echo Park to Silver Lake to Eagle Rock and a number of other places in between, I began to see an intricate weave develop.

Cedric, the African from Texas and Henrique, the African from Brasil, became twin figures with many things in common, to my slow brimmed eyes.

They were both artists, gentlemen from a school so old that it was blown away when they graduated. Romanticists about life, natural brothers, Capoeiristas. Obrigado, Henrique. Obrigado, Cedric.

Capoeira was an excellent prep school for hooking up with D.J. Capoeira gave me the solid underpinning for understanding what comrades should be to each other.

D.J., the photographer, discusses a photo of a beautiful woman in a popular girlie magazine. "Look at that, that dumb-stupid expression on her face, the fried chicken look

124

in her eyes."

"Fried chicken look?"

"Yeah, you know, like her eyes have been fried in grease. Slick, dead. Aside from the fact that the photographer did a lousy job—check out how poor the lighting is—she doesn't bring anything to the set at all, no feeling, no emotion, nothing. The only thing she really has going for her is cheek bones, a wonderful pair of titties and a great ass. Other than that, she's a dud."

I peeked over his shoulder for years, absorbing the sense of what a visualist sees, exposes himself to.

I learned what "shooting" means. When D.J. said, "I shot her," or "I'm shooting tomorrow morning," it was a bit like hearing a top flight matador say, "I made two incredible kills yesterday." Or, "I'm hoping to make an incredible kill tomorrow."

Soon after I began to pay serious attention to what he was doing, I immediately saw the corrida en Nikkon.

Here we have the Photographer, who is totally dependent on spontaneity, but at the same time, must be the "matador," the director of the corrida, the leader of the fight.

The "toro" bursts from beyond the "doors of death" ("Puertos de muertes") fully grown, alive with misconceptions, crazed by pre-life.

D.J. (or one of his assistant emotions) sends the bullshouldered model before the picadores to receive something that will lower their emotional shoulder muscles for the "kill" ("the shoot"). He patiently explains how careful we must be at this puncture-juncture.

"Gotta be real careful. If someone has been tellin' her all her life that her face is perfect, she may not be open to any change of lipstick or eye shadow. I've had some who had gorilla make-up on their cheeks and didn't want to change. But, hey, that's my job. O.K.? and I'm on my job."

His, "quites" (key-tays) are masterful; he takes her (or him) away from what is necessary, to what is absolutely possible.

In the middle section of what has to happen, the "Faena" (no English translation possible), he takes his muleta/camera and performs statuesque "naturales" that leave his subjects strolling through their emotional paces as easily as though they were following a piece of chocolate cake through a garden.

A blurred series of rhythms will sometimes disquiet his reboleras (look it up) but there is never any mistake happening when he approaches his Moment of Truth, which is most often a second for him.

The figure is captured flirting with the world (because she is a world flirt). He is a world flirt, his tenderhearted sub-teenaged violinist in black/white collar is playing an intellectually demanding piece from the violin repetoire; his grasp of the mother and three daughters (lightskinned, but only important for racist American purposes) in their portrait reflects subterranean concerns.

The matador/photographer never completely allows the "subjects/bulls" to determine the nature of what the rhythm of the fight is going to be. If he does, he has lost before the fight starts.

D.J. "kills" logically. If the lighting is not right, or the "bull" has placed his withers in an awkward position for the "kill," or the moment is too "juicy," he pulls back and re-profiles.

Most of the "kills" are perfect, but some are not. And that's the way he lives his life. He realized, "centuries ago," that it was not going to be the perfect quality of his photographs that would grant him immortality, but his attempts to create time.

My brother, my brother, my brother, my brother, my brother. . . .

Chapter 10

I seriously want to get a reading before I deal with Ade. I be right back. It wasn't possible, everybody is out to lunch. No, that's not really true, they weren't out to lunch, I just don't want to run the risk of knowing the truth. I'll just stick with my observations and imagination.

The first thing you have to understand about Ade is that he smokes (unless a miracle has happened), he smokes these gassy smelling cigarettes that must have all of the known carcinogens (label that "deaths") in the Western world, constantly. He goes beyond chainsmoking. He even sat at his mother's bedside, while she was dying of cancer, smoking.

If there was ever a man running around proclaiming his love life and trying to commit suicide at the same time, he's our man.

If it were possible to state, categorically, that contradictions form the foundation for most of our characters, Ade would have to be considered a supercharacter. And he is.

He is the character who pollutes his lungs with smoke and inspects the glass doors of restaurants to determine if the place is worthy of his patronage.

Perhaps this is the litany—definition of a multi-personality.

He builds houses and destroys all of the bridges in front of him. The lecherous guy who can't bear to see a young girl taken advantage of.

The undependably-dependable dude who may very well be there when you need him.

Ade, the generous friend; a clear trait. It's impossible to figure out how this happened in the midst of the contradictions, but there it is. If you need it and he has it, it's yours. The problem is getting a hold of him.

He is a man with a headache, or, as befitting a multi-personality, a man with several headaches. I can testify (put my thumbs on my balls) to the fact that he causes one of his headaches by demanding more of himself than he has to give.

It's a bit like watching a hundred yard dash man run the mile in ten seconds flat. And feel disappointed because he lost.

The intellectual blazes out at odd times, not so much a steady fire, but rather the incendiary effusion of the arsonist. He leaves you feeling bar-be-qued when this element torches, rather than baked or broiled.

No one had, or leaves you with, a greater imagination to feed on than Ade. Hold your ears still for a few minutes and he can lay an imagination-pasture out in front of your grazin' head that could fill you up with sunlight and chlorophyl for days. One wonders where it all comes from.

The adventurous side would have offered the most adventurous explorer worlds to see, things to explore that none of them could ever have imagined. If ol' boy Columbus had had Ade aboard, we can be sure that America would now be called

Adeland.

His sense of adventure or imagination does not encompass style. He believes in being clean, of course, except for the inside of his body, but has this weird idea that clothes are not supposed to justify their appearance on the human body unless they've been washed a thousand times.

This belief leaves him looking always like someone who has just stepped out of a laundromat, with a cigarette tied into his lips.

He is the inconsiderate pig pen who leaves a trail of Ade trash (cigarette butts, fish bones, miscellaneous scraps of metal and wood) and expects that someone will follow him to clean it up. As a matter of fact he is willing to pay someone to do it.

Ade, the social activist, the outraged patron of the supermarkets, who shoots through with a camera to record the smudge marks of the plastic carry carts.

Ade, the creative lifestylist who, despite all that's been said that may sound negative, continues to live one of the most imaginative lives of anyone I know.

Today he is a rich man who does not have a lot of money, but he *will* have a lot of money in the near future because he cannot continue to live the way he does and not be money-rich.

Ade, above and beyond all of this, a beautiful brother.

"Unca' John," also known at one time as "Sonny Boy" and later, as "Sweetmilk." Or just plain "Milk" to his friends, has always inspired me.

I was inspired by his exit from the neighborhood gambling joint one humid summer evening, the one run by the red-haired sister across the street from my aunt's gambling joint. The word had been circulating for hours, " 'Milk' winnin' big. 'Milk' winnin' *real* big."

I will never forget watching him stroll across Washburne Avenue after breaking the house. The red-haired woman stood on the porch, smiling at his exit between pulls of angry smoke.

He could've been Billy Eckstine, Miles Davis, Jim Brown, Marcus Garvey, Joe Louis and Richard Wright all rolled into one. He had an aura.

He also had a collection of parasites on him. He passed out coins to the children (he gave me a dollar!) and loaned the men tens and twenties.

He gave the money out as though it was his to give, but not with any sense of condescension; it was his and he could do what he wanted with it.

I say there was something inspiring about it because his actions were Grand, Noble. A lot has been written about noblesse oblige 'n stuff like that, but no one has covered the grandness of a relatively poor man dispensing that kind of largesse.

I like to feel that I was privileged (being his favorite nephew from our generation) to be let in on the secret of that tradition.

A powerful blessing is laid on the head of a blood relative who can have a role model like that.

When we were both younger, this sense of knowing who he was helped me survive a bunch of grim times, those moments every Black boy growing up in the ghetto must face.

I'm talking about the "moments of truth" that find you without food, decent clothes, a clean place to sleep, hope.

He maintained those elements for us. He fed me (and my sister) Sunday after Sunday (and sometimes during the week). The warm memory of pork chops, cream style corn, biscuits, peaches in heavy syrup and other goodies (prepared by Alberta and then Velma—he had divorced his first wife before I became aware that he had a son) advice.

"Yeahhh, well, that sounds like a good thing to do."

He was inevitably positive. Maybe it's part of the mysti-

130

que that a gambler must buy into. I can't really say.

I lived with him for weeks, at one point when our little family was being wedged into too tight a corner, in the summertime, keeping him awake at night with dumb questions, blundering from one wave of inept feelings to another, trying to channel my love into some form of philosophical gratitude.

He left early to chip ice from the freezers in the Stockyards, leaving me with coins, angelic summer days in Washington Park, Sarah Vaughn, Billy Eckstine, "Lady Day," "Pres," Nat "King" Cole, the Orioles, authentic music.

I sat at the kitchen table of his rooming house, (community kitchen here for real), one summer and wrote my first feverish book.

I had no outline, no plan, nothing but a ream of paper that Mrs. (Dr.) Margaret Burroughs had laid on me with a little advice, "Take some time this summer, and write."

No outline, no character sketches, just fever and hormones. It was about what happened at the "Peps" on a Saturday night.

The "Peps," on 47th, near St. Lawrence, was *the* dance hall for us. People died to get in and some died to get out. We smoked reefers in the balcony and drank cheap wine before entering. If you couldn't do an extravagant version of the mambo or if you didn't know how to do "the Walk" backwards, you couldn' get a dance.

The atmosphere, between the giant speakers that pumped "Anabacoa" into our souls, was so sensual that many of us had orgasms dancing. This was during the era when the girls became a part of the boys and vice versa.

That's some of what the novel was about.

Rooms. He always seemed to be living in a room, something like a monk, in a way. It wasn't because he couldn't afford anything better, (he could've lived on his uncashed paychecks for a good lil' while)...no, it wasn't because he couldn't afford a fancy collection of rooms, I think it was something else. I think it was a matter of choice. I think he wanted to live in "frugal" circumstances.

It wasn't like the crazed people who'd always had too much and wanted to neglect it; no, none of that psycho-stuff. That wasn't the Deal with him.

I don't think he'd ever had too much but I do think that he was one of the few people I've ever known who knew when enough was enough.

In many ways his surroundings, his circumstances, his lifestyle was a Real reflection of him. He was lean, clear, African. Despite the fact that he was in America, there were no compromises to be made about these three facts; he was lean, (at 5'6", I never saw a paunch or symptoms of gluttony. He ate when he was starving and fasted 'tween times). His "clear" ruled out a whole bunch of murky behavior. He didn't indulge in foolish behavior and had nothing to do with people who obviously needed psychiatric consultation. And wouldn't accept help.

He knew when enough was enough, for himself. But he was a cornucopeia for us. From his rooms (the basement on Lake Park, the back room on 59th and Prairie Avenue) he poured gifts of love, money, advice, seasonings for a sensitive approach to life.

An African-American, a cool operator, he never allowed the limited circumstances of being an African in America, or being under the pressures of that experience to interfere with his calm, to turn him into a simple Black man.

A lifelong gambler who was never addicted, he had never held any hand that was not the winning hand. Cards, anyone?

132

Chapter 11

My father was the best manfriend I ever had. He was a perfect father. He was so good that I find myself talking more and more about him during these enforced Black matriarchal days.

When I mentally flick up on him, I automatically close my eyes, the better to see this cool coal-Black man in his beautiful clothes.

I was looking at Jean-Marie Emebe, (who lost to Virgil Hill) the prizefighter from Cameroon, the other day, and I thought...damn! He's as black as my father was.

Yes, beautiful African-Black man, ebony in motion, and proud of it.

In recent years I've often wondered how my father's side of the family reached the pinnacle of feeling proud of their Black asses in the middle of a time that was programmed for self-hate.

The wonder is increased by my mother's side of the family, which is Arkansas medium-brown snuff-colored, and equally-adamantly Black.

"How did y'all pull it off?" I asked one day.

"The Indians helped us do it," my old auntie told me.

"The Indians?"

"Yeahh, you gotta understand that the Indians was the first civilized people we came into contact with in this country. They didn't have no problems dealin' with where we was comin' from because we had a lots of stuff in common.

"We were comin' from West Africa, from Nature, and they understood that.

"I'm not gonna make a long drawn out story out of it, but I'm sure that when the first Indians were invited to the first Bembe, they knew what was happening. Thanksgiving confused them and messed them all up. When they finally figured out what *that* was all about, it was too late."

Back to Daddy.

I see Daddy (not father) in four distinct lights, and then another four lights. And then four facets more. He gleams in my memory, just as he gleamed in life.

His body gleamed. I remember the look of him as he tilted himself up on his elbow, his hairless chest glistening, looking me over. He had just finished serving five years and eight months for a $10.00 robbery.

He was the fifth brother and they nicknamed him "Honey."

He was a rumor and a legend to my five year old ears and eyes before I saw him in court. It was literally that cold.

One day I was born and the next-day memory, I was in court, listening to a lot of white folks' legalese, the gist of it being, "We're tired! We say. . .we're sick 'n tired of dealin' with this boy. We're gonna sock 'em away, give ourselves a vacation from the likes of him."

Five years and eight months. For a $10.00 robbery?!

So, I got to know my father in prison. I'm positive that he was the final distillation of the Lingam strength of five Mississippi brothers. When they hoisted me up across the glass Maginot line at Stateville penitentiary to kiss my father, it was like a festival happening.

I wasn't being taken to a beaten man, a criminal, a fool behind bars; I was being taken to observe a warrior in chains.

Sometimes I would look out of the bus window, on my way away from the beautifully landscaped Stateville pen, and swear to avenge his imprisonment.

I knew, at five years old, that he was being forced to pay too high a price for his crime. And I was going to avenge him. Idealism and the young, huh?

They took me to see him often, not fully understanding what I understood. Or maybe they did.

I sat beside my mother, my aunt, my uncle, my aunt's girlfriend, my other uncles, my emotions. I looked across the barrier (there were no metal detectors then) and I saw a beautiful man who was being forced to pay too high a price for being himself.

Incredibly, he helped me. When we kissed (it was permitted) and his full, rich black lips settled on mine for as long as circumstances permitted, he *made* me understand that we were Black men under siege.

I have drummed, been exposed to drummers, absorbed drumming, and understood that his kisses were like that.

He could, without a visible hint of anything convey to me that his kiss meant—I love you but they tell me you fuckin' up; Quit it!—without seeming to change the direction of the rhythm, he could "break" it in mid-rhythm and send it off into another six-eight without any visible emotion.

I'm aware of several people who went to visit him and simply would sit, staring in his face for 45 minutes.

Prison lasted a long time, even for me. When we got back

135

into the city (with my clean Sunday clothes) and I was allowed to go back out to play, I felt disoriented sometimes.

My friend Dicky, during some of this, would say, "Why so sad, man?" in his special language.

I couldn't cry because I hadn't mastered the emotions connected with death and seeing your Daddy ina coffin-jail. Dicky cried for me. The brother was too deep.

When I was ten and full of strange notions, he was freed.

We stared at each other for long periods. I can remember the breathless moments, the times when we were obviously wondering—"is this my. . .?"

Before prison time, he was a shadowy figure, perfumed and elusive. During the prison time, when I sneaked reading of his letters and learned sublime words like "erection" and "vagina" and "sensualities," he was an education in spirituality.

Like I said, prison time lasted a long time. There were whole days when I couldn't talk to anyone because I was in "solitary." There were other times when I was allowed to mingle with the general prison population and I had to guard my back.

My father gave life to a spirit who was sympathetic to him. I praise the Orisha for that.

He was released suddenly, unexpectedly. No one had counted or measured the days out for me. He was there and I had to figure out who he was, quickly.

He aided the process by suavely announcing, "I'm your Daddy." Dizzy Gillespie and Chano Pozo, playing "Cubop City" backed him up. And Nubian incense.

I was looking at this man, this writer, who had been writing letters that made my thing hard, who had stimulated an interest in the Afro-erotic that lives as I die.

Needless to say, he was a heroic figure for my psyche. No one had to tell me not to talk about ex-stepfathers, or ex-lovers, or whatever they had been. They were absolutely eclipsed by his appearance.

He stayed with us in the basement on Bowen Avenue for a while. I compute it down to the time frame that it took him and my mother to get their "joneses" worked down to manageable levels. Logically, sensibly, the children were considered last, as the newest members of what was happenin'.

It would be impossible to say exactly when the full impact of what he was about sank into me.

I can always recall the night I saw him in the basement on Washburne, surrounded by loving relatives, when he said, "Fuck God!" and lit a joint. And the incense was clearly in my nose.

The tribal fire stood still, its flares piercing our night, the oldest faces in the world turned to stone and then softened.

"Honey," had said, "Fuck God!" and he had to be prayed for, seriously. And they did pray for him, for days.

"Lawd in Heaven, Jesus God Almighty, please forgive the boy, he didn't know what he was sayin'; please God, please forgive him!"

"Fuck God!"

I never forgot it. The fucking of God and the lighting of the joint. While everyone sank back into the shadows, the flare of his match created a vivid mask, filled with hollows and nuances. I didn't simply have a Maker, I had an Artist for a Daddy, someone who was willing to defy the undefiable.

I got happy on the idea.

The realization that this fantastic Black man was my father, someone who could bring himself to say "Fuck God!" and force everyone to pray (secretly) for him was definitely my kind of guy.

He opened the gates for me, very smoothly, very coolly.

"These are women, they want to be loved, not fucked. Do you understand?"

137

"I'm not sure, can you show me?"

"Yes, of course, watch me."

And he did allow me to watch him. On one memorable occasion he allowed me to join him.

It happened at the Sutherland Hotel, 47th and Drexel Boulevard.

The rules weren't quite so stringent then, and if you put on a hip demeanor and gave every impression of being a jazz lover they'd let you in.

The Sutherland lounge was where we went when we needed a taste of Miles, a shot of Diz or some Sarah and Carmen. Art Blakely, Lee Morgan, Stitt, Max Roach, Ahmad Jamal and hundreds of other classicists would be waiting in the wings.

The place was beautifully designed for musicians.

Horseshoe shaped bar with the players up there, a live sound, the place habitually taken over by an aficionado that was so heavy that loud talking and other disrespectful behavior could get your ass kicked.

"Hey, you! Shut the fuck up! We came to hear Ahmad Jamal, we didn't come to hear you!"

I was just sitting there, nursing a gin 'n tonic between sets when I saw him. Or them, I should say.

Objectively, clinically, I studied the man who had materialized on the other side of the bar and the two women with him.

Medium tall, well built Black man. He could've been a welterweight for sure. Well dressed in a conservatively cut pin stripe, clean.

A Black man with coarse straight hair, real dark, with large, beautifully defined lips, a small cut in the right corner of his mouth.

I watched him accept the cherries that the two women took from their drinks and placed in his mouth. One was an Afro-

Polynesian goddess and the other was a Viking queen. He loved sweets and beautiful women.

The marijuana sheen in his eyes tightened into a joyful glitter when he spotted me. He signalled for me to come to his side. I went.

He had picked up these two airline stewardesses somewhere, they were in an overnight holding pattern, and he was out on the town with them.

Mona and Ingrid.

It was hip and arranged. He ran it past me. "You're a lucky young man this evening."

"Oh?"

"That's right. You got anything planned for this evenin'?"

"Naw, not really. I was plannin' to stay for the last set and then make it on in."

"Hang with me."

"O.K."

After the last notes died, two more gin 'n tonics later, we left the lounge and retreated to room 400. I knew that the fast track folks maintained residency in the Sutherland but I had never been priviledged to share anybody's hospitality.

It was a warm night, the kind of funky night that used to wake Southsiders up and force them to go over to the lake and stare at the water.

I watched him roll up the smoke while I flung out unexpected bits of wit. Incense and blue bulbs.

"Richard, your son has quite a vocabulary." Richard? O-well, he was being "Richard" for the night. Must be a reason.

He loved marijuana and was frequently high on it. I could always tell, when his eyes slitted up and his gestures became more languid than usual, he was high.

We had a little more gin and capped it off with the herb. The stewardesses began to take off.

"It's so hot, would anybody mind if I took off my blouse?"

He grandly waved permission and whispered to me, "Be cool, we gon' make these two beautiful babies beg for it." And lit another stick of Joss.

I was fascinated. These two beautiful women were going to beg for it? How was that going to happen?

After an hour of lovely kissing, feeling each other's bodies and smoking more dope, Mona came out of her clothes and right there in the middle of the floor, in her bright red bikini panties, started shimmering like a bowl of Jello.

"Dis da way we do it in Tahiti, where I come from."

We were slipping farther and farther away from shore.

Lascivious behavior started a lava flow.

Ingrid came out of another bag. She had studied ballet and gymnastics and could walk on her hands.

A beautiful blonde, nude, watching our reactions as she walked towards us on her hands, upside down. A Tahitian fire walker, shimmering like a million drops of sea water.

"Looks like now," he said in low voice. We allowed them to undress us, to hang our clothes neatly on hangers before we joined them.

Ingrid was the only one who could walk on her hands but we could all dance, slowly, sensually.

We made love. We made love in the front room, in the bedroom, the bathroom, standing up, laying down, upside down.

We made funny love; strokes being halted in midstream while waiting for the punchline.

"See how much fun this is, lots of people take this shit too seriously."

I watched him hold himself in a push-up position, attached to the Tahitian flame by the length of his dick, as her motions created the optical illusion of one shimmering woman becoming four. The incense smoke curled up in spirals.

We sat in the window, bunched into a warm quartet, buck

nekkid, sipping another gin, and watched the sun come up.

It had been a beautiful night and a gorgeous morning. He called down to the desk and requested another day.

When we finally parted, we left each other with the kind of feeling that people—men and women—rarely share.

We hugged and squeezed each other at the cab stand, as though we were comrades who had fought in a lovely war. And won.

Ingrid did a spontaneous back walkover, Mona shimmy-shimmied one last time and they were gone.

"We didn't get their 'phone numbers or anything."

"Don't worry about it, we'll see 'em again. Or more like them."

They called him "Honey," in that ol' fashioned Afro-Mississippi way, depending on the sound of the word to make something happen.

He made lots of things happen with women. They simply had to have their "Honey" and their "Honey" had to have them.

"I don't see nothin' wrong with havin' three or four women at one time, if you can handle it. I mean, who said we only supposed to have one woman? Probably some chump who couldn't deal with more than one at a time."

I'm certain that his ultra-radical sense of father-ness would've scandalized every segment of the population, black, yellow, red or white. But he was perfect for me.

"Don't sit around lookin' frustrated, go get yourself a girlfriend."

If he had to discipline (prior to Sutherland Hotel days) me for something, he'd make me do fifty squat jumps. Or fifty pushups. He never laid his hands on me except to embrace me.

He knew how to leave me alone, to provide deserted areas for me to dream in. At one point, he and Uncle John thoughtfully provided me with more area than I needed.

I was a high school sophomore and junior—senior with two fully furnished rooms of my own. I had the keys to both rooms and I had been given the schedule of their arrivals and departures.

My uncle was regular with his. He left early and got home late. And on the weekend, he might be on the Westside gambling. Daddy was a little more erratic. He might trip through at any time.

I jogged away from the crowds of boys and girls, nursing their Cokes and nibbling their fries, to my sanctuary. No High School for me.

On some dreary afternoons, feeling a melancholy that seemed to be in the air I was breathing, I would go into my uncle's room, place a load of Billie Holiday on the turntable, flop on the bed and cry. Or simply stare up at the cracks in the ceiling for a couple hours.

I took girls to the rooms, but fewer than suspected. I didn't want to share my solitude with too many people.

Willie Dell came to my father's room and kissed me under the blue light that he loved. Alice came to his room one breathless afternoon, hormones and parental oppression stimulating her to love harder than any teenage girl had ever loved.

She told me that she had never really listened to "Bird" before.

"I always thought that was somethin' the fellas did, when they went off 'n got high 'n stuff."

"You don't have to get high to dig 'Bird,' he'll get you high. Listen to this."

We listened to "Bird" and made ferocious-teenaged love all afternoon. He may have stood in the door and watched us for five minutes before discreetly closing the door.

"Oh my God! What did we do?"

"Let's git this nut first. . . ."

"Wasn't that your father?!"

"Yeahhh, but he's cool."

Fear and confidence drove our passions into a thirty second sexual froth. I'm sure he must've laughed aloud at the moan we made.

He was sitting in the community kitchen, smiling and joking with a lady, the good Gordon's gin filling their cups.

Alice approached him, half hiding behind me. "Hi, Mr. Hawkins," she said, her eyes downcast.

"So, this is Alice. How're you doin', girl? O.K., now you treat my son special, O.K.?"

"Uhh huh, I am. . .uhh, I mean I will."

He showered his special little lop-sided lover's smile on me and that was it. No dressing down, no moral speeches. Nothing but this beautifully approving smile.

It was good, wasn't it?

"Do you know what would've happened to us if my father had caught us? He would've shot both of us and then cut us up into little pieces."

"My Daddy ain't quite like that. He don't believe in all that bullshit."

My Daddy didn't believe in a whole host of things. He didn't believe in America, for example.

"This country ain't never gave me shit! I've either had to take it or find it."

He took what he could find, as often as he could. He was a thief. And, from time to time, he would stick someone up. Which made him a thief and a robber.

He told me how it was done but he never encouraged me to do it.

"O.K., now let's take the "grab bag" for example. You can go to any pawn shop and buy one of these suitcases that look like everybody else's. You can fill it with rags or something, to give it some weight.

If you're workin' with somebody, this is the way me 'n Willie do it. If you got a partner, you get him to stash the suitcase in a locker and then you pull it out later.

That way, if anybody is checkin' you out, they won't see your face around the bus station, the train station or wherever, too often.

O.K., you take the suitcase and sit it down next to the chump you want to rip off.

Thing you have to remember is that the average sucker don't remember what color socks they put on this morning. Or what color tie they're wearin'. Check it out.

O.K., you try to catch people when their attention is focused on something else. You know how people stare up at the schedule board in the train station? Those are the chumps you wanna hit. Leave yours and pick his up and move on.

His approach to the art of robbery depended also on diversionary actions.

"I'll put LuLu near the corner of the alley and when the sucker starts down the street, by the time he gets near the alley, I'll signal for her to start raisin' her dress up. By the time she gets it up to her pussy, I've run up behind the chump, pop him upside the head and we be gone!"

I never heard him talk about these activities as though he were boasting, it was all matter-of-factly put.

He had done time for crime and knew what the inside of the pen looked like, so it was no empty piece of advice he was offering when he said to the neophyte lawbreaker, "If you can't do no time, don't commit no crime."

He didn't want to work, to become a wage slave.

"Ain't but two ways to make money in this country; either your granddaddy left you a million or you take a million. I ain't *never* heard of a workin' man gettin' rich."

He went out suddenly, like a light. One day he was there,

144

laughing, blaspheming, slicking his hair down under a stocking cap, drinking, fucking, smoking reefers, robbing, stealing, and the next day he was dead, killed by a jealous woman.

In a way that was typical for him, he had wound up living in an apartment with two sisters and their mother. One of the sisters was the killer.

He didn't age, decline, change. He was taken out the way he went through life, with fire and sauce.

If he loved too many women, he would find himself cornered by one of them.

"What the hell is life without takin' chances?" If he drank too much, he would discover that euphoria was full of day-after headaches.

"I gotta leave that firewater alone, and just stick with reefer."

If he made a mistake, he would be punished out of proportion to the error.

"Five years and eight months in the pen. Next case!"

And on it went.

Some say that he was killed for being too sweet and when he died his grave became a honeycomb.

Chapter 12

Tanina, Iyalosha Tanina Shongobumni was like my Daddy
in some ways. Number one, they were both "drawing cards."
I've seen people in the Iyalosha's presence who didn't even
know how they got there. Or why they were there.

In addition to, and aside from everything else, she was a
fine little sister, beautiful too, but more fine than beautiful.

Let's get specific. . .fine is that ingrained thing, like logs
have a grain to them, offering information about how long
they've been around, and what they've been through.

Tanina's eyes were the deepest indication of her "Fine,"
and her body was what made her beautiful. Her eyes were
clear set, the white white, the other parts black; the nuances,
mysterious.

She had a small body; what was she? Five feet tall? With
generous Afroid hips, when she wasn't sick.

It was almost like looking at a Kalahari woman; during the

lean seasons her ass shrank.

And there were Indians interwoven. Since she was Mississippi born we can assume that the welcoming tribe contributed a helluva lot of her genes.

Small, shapely sister, a priest of Shango. But I'm jumping ahead of ourself.

I didn't know her when I wrote "The Voodoo Lady" for the Sears Radio Theater. I don't think I knew anyone who was righteously practising The Religion when I wrote the voodoo show.

Yes, I've always known people who were doing stuff that I didn't understand (because it wasn't Time yet) and praying to our Gods. And it was always there, but I hadn't probed.

The "Moment" was the catalyst for the radio show and I guess, time for Tanina. "Baba" Mike Cooke was living in her house, exploring California in his style, and had invited me to a couple bembes. I hadn't been able to make a one, it wasn't time yet.

"Odie, you wanna come to a bembe?"

"Yeah."

"Saturday, July 9th, 8 p.m."

And I didn't make it. All of this was happening in Tanina's House. And I was missing it.

The Heritage Ensemble (take a bow, Senor Bobby Matos) swiped my rebuttal (weak) away like a thief in the night.

Who was playing with him that night? The jet black brother in the white cap, who played congas like a magician and danced like a prince. The thick ankled, yellow sister who was so full of Osun (Oshun) that lovers immediately surrounded each other, the svelte conga drummer with the swan neck who asked for Guidance before every set.

I didn't know how deeply I was into the religious people until the intermission came.

I stood back, awed by the respect this little woman with

148

these various colored beads around her neck was being offered.

No fool, me, I realized I was near a core. We tripped out to the Thai place on Hollywood Boulevard after the set. I jotted down the Ileke's colors. . . .

I was fully and completely captivated by her Attitude by this time.

We drank the tea and ate the rice and I studied the Iyalosha. She was always dressed New World Afrikan. Or Afrikan New World. Which means that her sense of style and fabric brushed against the senses so pleasantly that the block-rot shit began to crumble as soon as you touched her.

Fortunately, I was not overloaded with block-rot shit. We hit it off.

She got to me with her laugh. I've never heard anything like it. I had never heard anything like it, and I don't expect to hear anything like it until the next thunderstorm. She didn't conceal, she revealed.

The laugh was crude and sarcastic, at times, melodic. There were other times when it was sweet, generous, lushly tinted with Black Awareness.

Mike, having served his purpose, whipped back into the East; I turned toward the Iyalosha. She became a valuable friend, her wit and strength a source of energy for me, and a number of other people.

We fed on her, ferociously. And she gave us all we wanted.

She was an upper upper-grade African-American culturalist.

"I really can't understand why Afrikan people in America persist in calling themselves black. We didn't come from 'black,' we came from Afrika. Every fuckin' nationality in this country knows how to correctly hyphenate but us.

"We got Boom-Boom-Americans, Bow Wow-Americans. Bim bam-Americans and I don't know what else, and then we get us and we're just 'blacks.' It's a bunch of perverted white shit!"

Her language and basic thang was Terry-hip and beyond, she had come from ignorant circumstances and educated herself.

"Some members of my family still can't figure why I don't celebrate Christmas. I stopped trying to explain. Those who know where I'm at know, those who don't have something to learn."

She was the first priest I had ever known who really took her job seriously.

"I am not a priestess, I am a priest. I am an Iyalosha of Shango and I mean it."

Like I said, her thang was Terry-hip, which meant you didn't have to tippy toe around her sensibilities. She was robust about her life and her love.

"Would you like a lil' honey in your rum?"

I often had the feeling, visiting her, going somewhere with her, or just hanging out, that I was in the presence of a great person.

This great person had faults. She could be bitchy, cantakerous.

"I don't know why people; I don't know why *you* don't want to do what I'm asking you to do. Everyone always expects me to do something for them but they never want to do anything for me."

There was a flake of truth in her statement, but only a flake; many people felt privileged to do something for her. But only up to a point. There were times when she wanted complete obedience.

She loved The Religion and our people and was solid in her devotion to both. Some people thought she was a racist because she loved herself; the usual suspects.

"Funny, huh? When a German says he loves Germany

nobody thinks anything is wrong, but if an Afrikan in America says she loves Afrika, everybody thinks that's kinda wrong. Weird, huh?"

We spent many nights talking about The Religion, about Capoeira, about the Berimbau, about life and blood.

"Why shouldn't it be called 'The Religion?' It *is* The Religion. If Afrika has been called the womb for the birth of mankind then it's obvious to me that 'The Religion' was born where the first people came to be.

"Voodoo, Voodun, Macumba, Catimba, Santeria, Umbanda, Candomble, 'The Religion'. Strange, I hear them talking about 'voodoo economics' and I realize they don't know a thing about voodoo. They would never say Methodist economics or Jewish economics. And if they really knew how to apply voodoo to their economics we sure in hell would be in better shape than we're in now."

The Orisha spoke to her and through her and those of us who were beneficiaries never doubted her abilities.

"Can you imagine anybody not loving the sound of the Berimbau? I was standing out on my front porch area yesterday, just strummin' and someone from upstairs shouted down—'Stop that fuckin' noise!' Can you imagine?! I kept right on playin' 'til I got tired."

She could piss you off too. It usually stemmed from a way she had of making an argument into a non-argument, in order to de-fang her opponent.

"We're not arguing, we're discussing."

She was going to add Capoeira to her talent list (a beautiful dancer, sharp, clean, rhythmic motions; a singer of traditional music, a writer) before she passed on. And she would have, given a few more months.

"I feel close to what Capoeira is about."

The writer surfacing was a real surprise. It was as though you had known someone who never cooked and then discovered that she was a world class chef.

She was always a storyteller but the writing gave her another dimension. People after me will have to evaluate her contributions, I can only say that I felt her works were excellent.

And suddenly, it seemed, she was sick, in the hospital, dying of cancer.

Strong little warrior. She had never indicated any of the pitiful symptoms that some people automatically fling out when they hurt. Maybe she had become a bit more irritable than usual but she never became pitiful.

Her three trips to the hospital were like full scale battles and she won all three of them. I saw doctors and nurses staring at her with a strange light in their eyes when they came into her room.

You could see them saying—*so,* this is the voodoo woman.

When she stood up and left the place a few weeks later (the first time), they were still saying, but in a different tone— so this *is* the voodoo woman.

She ate well and drank wheat grass juice but we still fed too heavily on her and in the end we consumed her. It was almost that simple.

As a man I never witnessed her as Shango, the man, the warrior, but it was obvious that she was as attractive to women as any deeply grained man would be. And you'd have to be a damned fool to be around her and not understand that.

In the end, the warrior stood with a spear in both hands.

"It's going to hurt like hell."

"Tell me one thing, Doc, will it help?"

"Maybe."

"What's the alternative?"

"Certain death."

"Let's go for it."

I know, for many of us, who had been stumbling around, looking for an indigenous spirituality, she was sheer enlightenment.

For the Afro-culturalists, a gem of a professor and for the serious souls, a deep well.

It's New Year's Day on Santa Monica Beach, marine clear, brisk, almost sunny.

We are there to salute Yemanya, the five of us. We have baskets of beautifully arranged gifts, the mood is solemn, respectful, but not tense.

The songs were sang, the words said, the gifts offered. As we plodded back across the sands to our cars, I looked back to see an astounding sight.

In the space where we had just been standing a dozen people had suddenly materialized, ravaging the offerings that the ocean had towed into the water.

The impression they made was of vultures descending.

"Don't look back, Odie," she said, "don't look back."

And I haven't since then. Modupe, Iyalosha.

Chapter 13

Casey, Mr. Chickens, would probably have had a serious problem with the Iyalosha Tanina Shongobumni. Or maybe not. Maybe each of them would've understood the use that each of them made of chickens.

The Iyalosha used them as sacrifices and Casey used them to make money, as an entertainment.

Casey, or Mr. Chickens, as most of us who lived through his era called him, was not a personal friend. He wasn't someone I hung out with. Or drank rot gut wine with or talked nasty about girls with.

He was the familiar sight that warmed us in the winter, and inflamed us with delight during the hot months.

I always felt that the brother was doing something else other than what he seemed to be doing. It seemed to me that his stuff was being carried on at a spiritual level that eclipsed our thoughts.

Fix him in your head. Mr. Chickens, a tall, dark, goat-whiskered-Pre-Ras Tafarian-haired dude with obsidian eyes, striped at the corners by ghetto squint lines, shuffling back and forth in an overcoat that looks like an Afghan rug, at least 2,000 years old, the cord of a play telephone dangling around his neck, entwined with the body of a Baby Jane doll, looking alive, at times.

He recites a Montuno-Son of sheer poetry as he puts six mangy, scroungy, toothless, dirty, funky chickens through their paces.

"One dime, one show!" he calls out. His appeal is personal, profound. One has the feeling that he'd be saying and doing the same damned thing if he were at the South Pole, spoiling the penguins. Or the icebergs.

"One dime, one show!" he calls out to the assembled and the disassembled, "one dime, one show!"

We used to argue. . . .

"That motherfucker ain't doin' nothin' but some sophisticated beggin'!"

"Call it what you will or may, it's workin', ain't it?!"

"One dime, one show!" he calls out, oblivious to a ringside of fifty or a junior quartet.

"One dime, one show!" he calls out one final time, his own sense of time giving him the STARTCUE.

He uses a patient little baton to help two of his chickens up onto the length of the rope that he has attached to a grill at the edge of the sidewalk. We all look on, buggy eyed.

He slowly pulls the rope taut and suddenly the chickens are doing a Wallenda across the abyss of half a sidewalk, as he clucks a constant stream of poultric love signals to them.

"One dime, one show!" he sings out in his rich baritone.

After a tense moment or two, he eases the chickens down from the "high wire," squatting on his ancient heels as the chickens huddle around him, quick pecking in perfect order at carefully placed bitlets of corn kernels.

"One dime, one show! One dime! One show! No dime, no show!" he sings out periodically, totally involved with the ways of his chickens.

Sometimes, one of the adults would drop a dime on the ground. One of Mr. Chicken's chickens (six, remember) would quickly waddle over to pick it up and quick step it over to Mr. Chickens.

Reinforcing his training sessions, he would give the well indoctrinated chicken a few special bits of seed. Or was it cabbage?

It was all done in such a smooth, cool way. "Make 'em dance, Mr. Chickens!" one of us would sing out.

"Yeahhh, make 'em dance!" the Afroid chorus would respond.

"Just the females!" one of the adult soloists would say.

"How you gon' tell the difference?" a counterpoint soloist would ask.

"Bruh Chickens know the difference!" the counter-counter point would call out, usually in a tone that none of us children understood.

Mr. Chickens stared opaquely at the comedians around him and then, suavely, tapped his baton, clucked to his hens (five of the six) and they would riffle into a semi-straight chorus line, shuffling back and forth.

Mr. Chickens would begin to cluck a guanguanco tempo to them. The show would last a hot two minutes. "One dime, one show! One dime, one show! No dime, no show!"

By this time, we, the "other" chickens, unable to bear the idea of no mo' shows, would rain dimes down. The chickens clucked and picked up and carried dimes to him like bird dogs. No pun intended, of course.

"One dime, one show! One dime, one show! No dime, no show."

We could never figure out when enough dimes had been collected to promote a show, or when the chickens had become bored with our shit. Or whether Mr. Chickens, satisfied that he had presented the best show in town, would be ready to move on.

In any case, we felt that we had lost a friend when we didn't see him anymore.

Needless to say, whenever I see a live chicken (a rare species these days) I ask, "Hey, my friend, have you seen your friend, Casey?"

No need to bullshit here in another sector of the Animal Kingdom, Brother Yusef, no chicken, almost didn't make it.

If he had been a chicken, struttin' 'n cluckin', I would've understood what to do about him from the git.

But he wasn't a chicken who would strut proudly in his own shit, or allow himself to be clucked to the feeding bin or taught to pick up dimes and bring them to the master; no none of that boogie woogie.

Yusef was a cat. And without making a long deal of it, I must say he became my alter ego. But it took time.

Yes, Lawd, it took time. When he first crept into my life, as a three month old ball of inky fur, I had serious doubts about the possibility of him surviving my hangups.

It had to do with this strange habit he had, of rubbing his body against the side of my face in the middle of the night.

I lost count of the number of times I awoke in a nightmare-rage, re-experiencing the rat plagues of my ghetto youth, to brush his little ass out of the bed. And, a couple times, against a nearby wall.

He was a fierce little animal who loved to claw and scratch. My legs and hands seemed to be special targets. It was all very cat-like.

We became friends, cat-like, in his teenage years. I slowly

began to realize that I had a peerless pimp living off of me. And he was addicting me to his style.

He was not going to fetch my shoes to my bedside, gallop up to me with the daily newspaper dripping from his mouth. Or do any such thing that could be misconstrued as doggy ass behavior.

No, he was going to prowl the fences and rooftops of the neighborhood, shiffing for foreign piss stains and elusive pussy. And rest up in the sun the next day so that he could go back out the following night.

It came to me like a shot one afternoon, watching him folded up in the peculiar-to-cats yoga posture, that he was a god. And that he had always been a god.

He caught my awed expression and stared back at me, through me and beyond me for a full minute, as though to reaffirm my thought.

My lessons were taken to a new level from that day forward. It seemed as though I had passed some kind of cat test.

One evening, tired and frustrated with an idea I was trying to crystalize, I aimed at least ten balled up pieces of paper at a nearby wastepaper basket, a common occurance in the pre-high tech days of writing.

I saw his shadow, which was the same color as his body, slide past my chair. He casually padded over to the balls of paper and began to bat the balls around, doing what we always call "playing."

Yes, "playing" might be one description of it, but it would never come close to the terrible speed of that paw, the liquid grace of this small panther, the real sense of watching a wild animal pretend to be "domesticated." If he bothered to pretend anything.

He batted one of the balls of paper over to my shoe and coolly squatted to watch me.

"Pick it up, fool," he seemed to be saying. And, pointed

to the paper with his left paw.

The idea was scribbled in my handwriting but I couldn't recall having written it. It was the idea-shape that I had been looking for.

I looked up grateful to him for helping me, but he was gone and I never saw him again.

I often feel that Brother Yusef wanted to end our relationship at a peak of something.

And he did.

Chapter 14

They had flown in from all points of the compass, they were
'My Menfriends' in living color; they were meeting in the
African Room of one of the Southside's largest hotels.

The meeting room was dominated by a round conference
table that offered space for fifty, a fully loaded bar nestled
in two corners of the room and a sideboard literally groaned
from the weight of catered goodies.

'My Menfriends' was in session, Brother BoBo in the chair.

"Awright, everybody, let's come to order! Hey! Cool it!
O.K.?! Now then, as you all know, we have gathered here
tonight, 12:00 midnight seemed to suit everybody pretty well.
We have gathered here to deal with what the brother done
wrote about us, wid his sneaky ass. . ."

"I heard that!"

"Shut the fuck up, R.B.! 'Fore i jump down there on your
skany ass, you a jive ass motherfucker and I never did dig

161

you, even when we was growin' up together."

"Whoaaa! Just a minute, Mr. Chairman, I thought we were 'sposed to be having a serious meetin' about what the brother said in his book?"

"You got that right, but that don't mean we can't speak the truth about how we feel about other things."

"I heard that!"

"Shut the fuck up, R.B.!"

"Mr. Chairman, BoBo, I have a question."

"The chairman recognizes brother Herb. Go 'head, Herb."

"Well, the first thing is, I'd like to be clear about why we're having this meeting. Are we having the meeting to say something about what he said about us? About something we don't agree with? Or are we just here to have a few drinks and let off some steam?

"Personally, I think he did a fabulous job; he didn't lie on nobody so far as I can tell. What's the beef?"

"What's the beef?! Shit! We got a whole lot to beef about! I wasn't pleased worth a damn with all that b.s. he said about me."

"R.B., if you wanna say something you have to raise your hand and be recognized by the chairman, just like everybody else."

"I did raise my hand, man."

"Did I recognize you?"

"You should have if you didn't."

"Heyyy, c'mon, let's stay on the track, you two dudes can deal with that personal shit later on."

"You right, Herb. Go 'head, R.B., let's hear your skany ass."

"Well, the first thing I wanna say is that I don't think he should've wrote the book in the first place. I mean, the way I look at it, he just exploited us. He took everything he knew about us and put it in a book and what do we get out of it?"

"Uhhh, can I answer that, Mr. Chairman, Bo'?"

"The chair recognizes 'Long Dick' Woods."

"I'm gon' be up front about my feelings about what the brother wrote about me, I dug the shit outta every single word! That's the first plus for me, the fact that I dug it.

"The second thing is what it did for my rep. One of the best things in the world is to have a good rep."

"Awww, you just sayin' that because his book helped you get a lot mo' pussy."

"I was already swimmin' in an ocean of it before the book came out, R.B."

"Let's knock off the cross rappin'! Let's stay on the track. I think we've finally come to a point here.

"What we want to do is have everybody offer their opinions about what they think of My Menfriends and then, depending on whether we agree or disagree, let's vote on whether we should send the brother a letter of appreciation or whether we should get together and stomp his ass into the dirt, after we've broken his nose, his thumbs, caved his chest in and knee-capped him. What say y'all?"

"Yeahhhh!"

"Nawwww!"

"Good! The yeahhhs have it. The chair recognizes the brother over there."

"Uhhh, this is brother Dicky and he can't talk. I mean, he don't speak regular words, but if you give him your un-divided attention, he *will* be able to get his point across."

Dicky the childhood friend from Washburne Avenue, walked slowly to the front of the room, carefully orchestrating the pantomime he was going to use, to "speak" about his friend who became the author of "My Menfriends."

He swept the gathering, with several elegant gestures, into a world that he had shared, one that was dead, bulldozed and stinkin'.

He led them, with motions that were utterly hip, through the trash heaped alleys of the Near Westside, his eyes, lips, cheeks, chest, hands, arms and soul performing what someone later called, "A Ghetto Boy's Concerto."

He "explained" the fears they once shared, the pleasures they lived through, the awkward moments of having no one to appreciate the depths of their love offerings. Or their despair.

He "sang" the songs they'd sang and told the jokes they'd told, wordlessly.

The cognoscenti leaned forward to share the cool pantomimed watermelon feasts of those blistered days, days that leaked humidity and funk.

They sprawled in their seats, the echoes of ancient moods pulling them back; they heard, from a man who couldn't speak, what he felt about a man who had been his friend when they were boys in a Black world.

Several of the "Menfriends" spontaneously applauded at the conclusion of his "testimonial." Dicky responded with a gravely suave smile and glided back to his seat.

"Well, he can say all that if he wants to, but I don't happen to agree."

A quartet of good ol' boy types, conventioneers to the Big City, blundered through the doors of the meeting room, took a series of stunned looks at the "Menfriends" and blundered back out.

"As I was about to say, before we was so rudely interrupted, the chairman recognizes Leo, or is it Tony de Medrow now?"

"It's neither one, it's Nick Bantuchi. . . ."

"Oh wowwww! You gotta be kiddin'. . . ."

"I don't see anything strange about changing a name. Why can't I be Bantuchi, if I wanna be?"

"It's cool with me, Leo, you can call yourself Mr. Dog Nuts, if you want to."

"Awww c'mon y'all, let's cut the crap and stay on track here."

"Righteous on!"

"Well, what do you want to say, Leo?"

"I told you once, man, my name is Nick. . . ."

"Awright, man, your name is Nick. O.K.?! O.K.?!"

"Thank you, Mr. Chairman. Well, the first thing I have to say is that he wronged the fuck outta me! He made me out to be somebody who was heavy into *self-hatred* because I didn't want to be bogged down by that stupid ass name that my parents gave me.

"I was never the name they gave me, I was somebody else when I landed on the planet. You dig? When I went into the business world, the first time, I became Roger Fawnsworth V, the, uhh, VI, sorry 'bout that."

"Who you supposed to be now?"

"I just told you, I'm Nick Bantuchi and I don't appreciate what he had to say about me. That's all I have to say. I vote we take him out!"

Dicky chorus-led the uproar that followed. The chairman gaveled the assemblage back to order.

"Everybody shut the fuck up! We got a right to have differences of opinions, even if all of us don't agree with that! Let's git on! The chair points to the brother over there with the African cap cocked ace deuce."

The man with the African cap cocked ace deuce, stood and, despite the fact that he was not particularly tall, seemed to cast a large, warm shadow over the gathering.

When he spoke, his voice rich with the accent of an Afro-Cuban birth, his sentences had the effect of quinto solo.

"He is a good writer, no? He's always tryin' to tell the truth, right?!"

After a couple rhythmic sentences he had provoked a tonista/chorus effect, claves squeezing in from left and right.

165

"So now, some people are not satisfied, huh? So, what is he 'sposed to do? Give up hees vision for someone who had no vision? If those persons who are dissatisfied with what he had to say about theem, then they should write thee book they want. Remember, my freeends, we only com' theees way one time so we must be ready to do the berry best we can. I think he deed the best he could wid dee best he had to work weed."

"Thank you, thank you for your comments, brother. . .awright now, whose the white guy wid his hand up?"

"The name is Bloch and I have to agree with Mr. uhhh. . . ."

"My name is Armando Peraza."

"I have to agree with Mr. Peraza, he did the best he could with what he had to work with. I could quibble with some of the structural things, but I'm going to go out on a limb and say. . .it wasn't a bad effort.

"The one thing I've always known about his work is that it showed evidence of a very personal agenda."

"What the fuck's that mean?"

"What the fuck's what mean?"

"Personal agenda."

"Well, let's just use the simple form and say he can't be accused of being glib, he takes his subject matter seriously and tries to give it his deepest shot. What I like about him is that he remains a student of his art."

"I still say he did me wrong!"

"Awright, Leo, chill out!"

"My name is Nick!"

"Awright, Leo-Nick, chill out! You had your turn, let's keep the ball rolling. Who's next?!"

"I am. They used to call me 'The Toe' and, as I look around this room, I can see dudes I used to run up 'n down the court with, dudes I used to hang out on the corners 'n shoot the shit with. Or sing. I thought he told the truth about me."

"Of course he told the truth about you, man, he told his version of the fuckin' truth about all of us. . . ."

"Have you been recognized by the chair, Big Man?"

"My name is Gordon Bussey and no, I have not been recognized by Your Chairship. Are you belatedly exercising your right to perform that function at this time?"

"Yeahhh, I am. You have the floor."

"Fine. Now then, as I was saying. . .he told, related, his version of the truth about us. My only complaint, seriously speaking, is that my section was miserably short, all things considered."

"That it?"

"If I think of anything else that needs to be said, I'll request Chairship recognition."

"Thank you, sir."

"Oh, one other thing; Peace."

"The brother with the camera, your turn."

"My brothers, my brothers, my brothers, my brothers. . .I am D.J., the freelance photographer and I must say that I was quite pleased to be able to read 'My Menfriends'.

"Now then, having said that; if everyone here will follow my directions, we'll have a group shot to end all group shots."

The assembled group was pushed and prodded into the most photogenic position possible and several historically interesting photographs were taken. The meeting went on.

"Steele here. I don't recall the night he spoke about, the night he helped me get to the bus station, but I'll tell anybody, I'll never forget Henrietta, never, never, ever."

"Dig that!"

"The chair recognizes the brother with the black silk suit."

"My name is Bo' Felt. I have to say, at this point, it's a real pleasure to be here. To exchange points of view about someone that I've watched go through as many changes as a dude can go through and still maintain.

"I'm not going to go off into what he said about me, that's neither here nor there. In other words, I'm saying this: the most important thing, from my perspective, is the fact that he offers us psychological studies of ourselves that we might not ever have received.

"If we keep that simple fact in mind I think it'll be real hip to pick up 'My Menfriends' ten years from tonight and check out who we all were and what we became. I could see a sequel happenin', maybe he could call it, 'My Ladyfriends'."

"Movin' right along, Mr. George Jackson."

"Well, as most of you all know, we went to high school together but I didn't really get to know the dude 'til we got into Junior College together. He was always kinda wild, a bohemian, I should say. . .

"I tried my best to work with him, to try to steer him right but I guess I failed."

"Awww c'mon, George, you didn't fail! You just didn't succeed."

"Awright, that's enough of that. Go 'head, brotherman, your turn."

"Thank you, baby. The name is Terry and I'm goin' to make my remarks brief 'n to the point. The brother is a good spirit, ya' understand what I mean? And good spirits are a hard find. I made him the Godfather of my oldest son, need I say more?"

"That says it all. The chair points its finger at Palmer."

"Thank you, sir. The first thing I'm gonna say here, and those who disagree too strongly can meet with me out back, after this is over. Like George here, I knew Hawkeye in high school. We played hardnosed football under Coach Jim Brown, on the gravel, folks, *on the gravel*.

"I said we played football on gravel, my friend, and that's what I mean. I think this book·is a direct reflection of that experience."

"In what way?"

"Like how to get down to the nitty gritty right quick!"

"Thank you for your comment. What do you have to add to that?"

"Just plain Ralph here, unless I decide to become an astrophysicist on the spur of the moment."

"Uhh, what was it you wanted to say, brother?"

"I'll be as brief as possible because I see we have a number of people waiting to speak their piece.

"Gotta start off by saying that I've shared about as much madness with Hawk as anyone here; as I mentally review, some of it made lots of sense and some of it made no sense at all. But I think that's one of the plus signs we have to become involved with, if we're going to live creatively productive lives.

"I've had people accuse me of being too creatively productive, because they thought they couldn't buy into it.

"You show me someone who is unwilling to buy into creative productivity and I'll show you a mean-spirited, shallow-minded essence of a person. We've got to get away from thinking what the books want us to think, that's what kills off original thinkers.

"Let's take a close look at some of the really original thinkers in the world; Hilda, a St. Bernard we owned for a time—Bless her deceased St. Bernard soul!—was an original thinker. Her thinking was so original that I can't even begin to give you an idea of what she was thinking about most of the time. Now that's what I call original thinking!"

"It's gettin' kinda late, brother Ralph, could you get to the point?"

"The point? The point I'm tryin' to get to is unattainable. All I'm tryin' to say is simple; all writing, no matter how real it is, is ultimately fictional, simply because it's in print and people don't live print lives, people live real lives. But I thought 'My Menfriends' was real, 'specially the part about

169

me 'n Palmer."

"Ade, can you add anything to that?"

"I could add a helluva lot, but I'm not going to. I met the author through my mother and I have to state, in all fairness, I don't really think he knew me well enough, or long enough, to say some of the things he said.

"Of course, some of the things he said are correct, up to a point, but a lot of what he says is not quite on the mark. In any case, I'd advise everyone to go out and buy the book, it'll help sales."

"Now then, I can't really make myself believe that a black cat, a real black cat is going to give a testimonial but. . .Mr. Black Cat?"

"Meeeeeeooooooowww, O.K., for the sake of those who are not hip to 'Catese,' I'm going to say what I have to say in plain English.

"Let's let the record show that when we first hooked up he didn't dig me and I definitely didn't dig him. I attribute the whole misunderstanding to his ghetto background. To him, anything purring up to him with fur had to be a rat.

"I understood where he was coming from but he was very slow to deal with my point of view. I don't know if he ever did, in any case. . .meeeeow purrr meeeoooww purr purr purr. . . ."

"And your name?"

"They nicknamed me Yusef, but my real name is purr purr meowww Jones."

"Thank you, brother purrr purrr meowww Jones A.K.A. Yusef."

"I don't have to raise my hand, I was his Daddy."

"Now we really gittin' into it, Odie Sr."

"You got that right. I'd like to say, without any reservations whatsoever, that I'm as proud as a father could be that most of the stuff that I laid on him stuck. He could've wound up being a funky chump and bought into the set up that was willing to grant him naked slavery, but he didn't. He went straight to the honey and if y'all don't know where that's at, shame on you!"

"Next person please, we're runnin' outta time."

"They've called me 'Sweetmilk,' they've called me 'Sonny Boy,' they've called me 'Milk.' And some people have called me some names I don't want to repeat. I'm his uncle. But none of that matters. What matters is that he has always shown the heart and guts to do what he set out to do.

"I guarantee you, if you look at the whole thang, you'll see him saying something about us that's been needed sayin' for a long time."

"J. C. on the soapbox here. Say, what're you guys doin', freakin' off or something?! Lookit! This guy has puffed us all up. He hasn't said anything that anyone would be ashamed of reading on the shitter walls.

"Hell! If somebody wanted to be pissed off about what was said about them, it would be me. The point is this!—You don't accuse one section of an engine of any crime until you investigate the integrity of the whole system.

"I see a bunch of puzzled looks. O.K., lemme take a couple hits on my ouzo here and I'll try to straighten this out. Look at it this way, he's showing us, in this book, something we didn't know about ourselves and I don't see anything wrong with facing that reality.

"You look at yourself in the mirror when you shave, don't you? He's just being a mirror for us. No problem here."

"What's that you're drinkin'?"

"It's ouzo and if you didn't put in on it you can't have none."

"Thank you very much, for nothin'. O.K., I see two hands over there, I'm going to recognize both of y'all at the same time."

"My name is Henrique."

"My name is Cedric."

"Well, who is goin' to speak first?"

Henrique/Cedric, together: "We're not going to say anything, we're going to sing a song."

"Sing...a...song?"

"Right, sing a song."

"Go 'head...."

> *Parana eh*
> *Parana eh*
> *Parana*
> *Vo mimbora pra Bahia*
> *Parana*
> *Tao cedo nao renho ca*
> *Parana*
> *Se nao foi essa semana*
> *Parana*
> *E a semana qui passo*
> *Parana*
> *Parana eh*
> *Parana eh*
> *Parana*
> *Do no escondo a ponta*
> *Parana*
> *Ninguem sabe desata*
> *Parana*
> *Parana Eh*
> *Parana Eh*
> *Parana*
> *Chique-chique mocambira*
> *Parana*
> *Joga pra cima de mim*
> *Parana*
> *Eu so braco de mare*

Parana
Mas eu so mare sem fim
Parana Eh
Parana Eh
Parana
O digero, digero
Parana Eutambem so digero
Parana

At the conclusion of their song, most of "My Menfriends" stared at the singers as though they were circus freaks. The chairman broke the spell with a lusty, "Wall, alll riggght! That was alright!!"

J.C. held his uozo glass up in a toast. "Here's lookin' at you kids."

The chairman, semi-anxious to bring the whole business to the voting stage, scanned the members to make certain that he hadn't missed anybody. "Well am I going to be allowed to speak my piece or not?"

The Chairman subconsciously rubbed his eyes, almost caricaturing surprise. His startled look was cloned twelve times. They all took careful note of the small, finely designed sister standing on the chair, six places to the left.

She wore an intricately designed headwrap, a white lace, West Afrikan wrap around, and an ileke.

"After everybody has stared at me long enough, will the chair recognize me?"

"Oh, sorry 'bout that. The chair recognizes the sister."

"Modupe."

"Can I ask you one question before you begin?"

"Of course, what is it?"

"I...uhhh. I can't seem to remember you being here, up to this very moment. Where...?"

"I was here, you just didn't see me. Can I continue?"

173

"Please, go right ahead."

She looked around at the members of the 1st Annual Convention of "My Menfriends," slowly deliberately, a glitter in her deep brown eyes, as though she were cataloguing each face for future reference, a glistening aura flickering around her head.

Her son held his head down respectfully, staring at the table in front of him. She reached for the coconut shell basin half filled with water that materialized in front of her, and with a delicate sprinkle from her fingertips, from coconut basin to sprinkling fingers, she spoke. . . .

"The author of 'My Menfriends' asked me to be here, to offer blessings for this gathering. I accepted his invitation and I am here, as you can see.

"Now then, what I want each person to do is say, answer Ahshay, as I offer my blessing. Can you all say Ahshay?"

The ahshay that they gave in response to her request was a bit ragged.

"Let's put a little more feeling into that Ahshay."

"Ahhhshayyyy."

"That's much better. Alright, let's have it understood, first of all, that we are here tonight, not just simply to give opinions about a book, but to speak to the spirit of what inspires an African-American writer to write."

"Ahhhshayyyy."

Her graceful fingers flicked droplets of water from the shell into the air in front of her.

"We want to give thanks to the Orisha, to our Ancestors, for giving some of us the courage and ability to pick up the pen. And the sword."

"Ahhhshay. . . ."

"We honor and cherish the memory of all those who came before us, who wrote with their souls and lived Ourstory in their blood, sweat and feelings. . . ."

"Ahhhshayyy."

"We are able to look at this world with a clearer vision, knowing that those who came before us, who prepared the way, knew what the real deal was, and passed that knowledge on to those of us who were willing to listen."

"Ahhhshay. . ."

"We are ancestors of those who will someday become ancestors and we *will* them the right to be whole, to be unique, to be prosperous, to be healthy, to be incredible, to be beautiful, to be stimulating, to be soulful, creative, to be African. . . ."

"Ahhhshayy. . ."

"We are a unique spiritual force in this world, and we owe more than money to the developers of this force. We honor and respect them."

"Ahhhshayyyy."

"On this Earth, in this world, and all other worlds, I offer prayers that we will have many meetings of many 'Menfriends,' womenfriends, animalfriends, plant friends, friends period.

"Ahhhsahyyyy."

"I pray that 'My Menfriends' will remember that Iyalosha Tanina Songobumni was here and offered Ahshay."

"Ahhhhshayyyy."

'My Menfriends' stared at the coconut shell half full of water and the empty chair in front of it.

Dicky stood solemnly and pantomimed, it's all over, there's nothing more to be said or done.

Ahhhshayyy. . . .

Epilogue

In the beginning, when it seemed that the game of writing contained more magic than I felt capable of dealing with, I slid the words onto the paper without any real notion of what I wanted them to do. I got down into it with flaring nostrils, determined to fill up as many pages with as much stuff as possible.

No one pointed the way or laid the rule book open in front of me, I was on my own and I didn't know whether I loved it or not. The options were bewildering.

I could go left, right, up, down, in, out or nowhere; it all seemed to depend on me. Of course, since that time, I've grown to understand that the freedom I thought I had was an illusion.

It didn't take many years of sweat and mistakes to learn that my writing life, my creative life, was being governed by laws more serious and stringent than most of those designed by the worlds' governments.

The damned pressures from every angle closed in on me; I was going to be an African-American writer and speak to all the elements of that genetic printout. In addition, I was going to have some say-so about what was happening in every area of my experience. I was going to write about love, lust, suffering, joy, grief, pathos, geopolitics, animals, plants, the moon, America. I was going to take the dangerous step of attempting to understand myself and others.

After the first glitter of the illusion faded, I realized that I was not totally prepared to write about half of the things I felt that I wanted to write about. I had not read enough.

I had lived enough, but it hadn't been the kind of life designed to help the mind come to grips with the minds that gripped it. I had to start all over again, from scratch, in a sense, to push dew dripped dreams and fancy ideas off into a distant corner.

My beginning was once again a fitful start. It took place in front of the bathroom mirror, silently asking my image to tell me, to explain why I was doing what I was doing. And did it really matter?

The image lied to me faithfully, for years. It would unlock the question and hide the key from me. Or it would toss the key at me and hide the lock. Or it would simply lie and tell me whatever my eyes seemed to be asking for.

It became necessary to look into other mirrors, ask others' questions, develop a method that would truthfully let me know what the real deal was.

The art of enthusiasm was replaced by the study of a craft. I slowly began to realize that I was preparing my head for a series of battles that were going to take place on so many fronts at one time, in so many places, that I would have to be fighting, even when I slept.

The challenge was a great one, but the second I dealt my

hand, allies started filing out of the closet. This one offered discipline, passion, imagination, that one taught mental Capoeira, evenmindedness, an appreciation of Death and its opposite, others, other things.

I no longer needed to stare into bathroom mirrors, asking the wrong questions.

Gradually the words began to sound like the sound I had in my head, and they began to make the impressions I wanted them to make, in other heads. I think.

There were mornings, in the beginning, when I wrote 300 page novels for breakfast and twenty page short stories for lunch and a serious article or two before the day was over. I lusted after what was compelling me to scribble, scribble, scribble.

And the lust exhausted me. There were days when I didn't know what day it was, or what time or where I had eaten my last meal. Secretly, I was insane for long stretches, barely making the correct responses to the world's questions, waiting patiently for sanity to return so that I could write some more.

An ally whispered the secret of mental salvation in my ear, forcing me to abandon momentary lapses of the mind. I was all set. But problems remained.

The outside, looking in on me, would not/does not accept my plea for a humane experience, because of the obvious benefits to be snared by remaining inhumane. Just another battle on another front.

But now I was set, I had formulated enough game plans to keep enemies and friends occupied. My life had developed enough purposes to keep me occupied.

I wandered for awhile after coming to grips with this realization, the lust that had exhausted me was loosening its grip, I could relax sometimes and even sleep.

As usual, in my third dream, one summer evening, the one

plan that I needed to enable me to channel all of the battles to one front for a while, and sleep more peacefully, came to me.

The dream revealed a tapestry and the threads were from the many strands of my life. Eight books would do the trick. I got busy immediately. *Ghetto Sketches* would satisfy the urge to explain the Near Westside of Chicago that had been bull-dozed under, re-ghettoized and still stank.

In *Ghetto Sketches,* the neighborhood was re-born, explored again, the unique characters allowed to speak in this gorgeous Black/African-American English that causes some of us to run across the street in foreign capitals (yes, Africa too) when we hear someone laugh in those tones. We want to talk with them, share warm looks at each other's mouths, do the do.

Chicago Hustle would give me the chance to do a serious character study of a man who could've been the president of any major league firm in this or any other country. And show why the society we live in will never allow such an even-tuality to occur. *Chicago Hustle* would allow me the oppor-tunity to go with the flow that I once knew best. The "fast people" immediately got on to what was goin' down and bought the last copy.

No, Baby Doom, it was not intended to be a textbook for the unhip, the uninitiated, the unslick, the uncool, the. . .well, you get the idea.

As much as I hated the idea, *Sweet Peter Deeder* had to be woven into the tapestry because he represented (in my opi-nion) a figment of the West African (transported) collective racial psyche that has not been given the objective considera-tion it must have, to be fairly shown.

We were not eliminated from the West African idea of polygamy because they eliminated West Africa from us. Never did believe it and had no need for Swedish sociologists to explain that. Or anything. *Sweet Peter Deeder* represents an aberration of the polygamous impulse, due to socioeconomic factors beyond his control. This is one of the reasons why I included a homosexual—Mayflower—in his stable.

Strangely, this is not something everybody picked up. Maybe, if the book was in hardback and cost $14.00, they would've.

I said, as much as I hated the idea of adding *Sweet Peter Deeder,* I had to. Because he is what the place we live in is, a pimp. And he personifies this perversion.

The Memoirs of a Black Casanova was an effort to set the collective psyche back in sync. It was (I felt) a well padded push back to Pussy. And if that needs any explanation beyond "Pussy," then shame on you!

Yes, of course, it has all been political, but *The Busting Out of An Ordinary Man* was *my* political statement. I feel that every African-American writer must, inevitably, just come on out and say—shit! I do not believe in George Washington (the one with the slaves and the wooden teeth) or the flag, or all the rest of the bullshit that makes immigrant white folks weepy. *The Busting Out of An Ordinary Man,* politically, is an effort-statement made to express the profound disgust that intelligent Africans in America have felt with/for the status quo.

I once heard a sister say, "I wish that the Native Americans had been in a position to grant us Second Class Citizenship."

Are you ever going to find that statement in a mainstream publication?

They were always on my case: "We're confused, motherfucker! You seem to be writin' about one fuckin' thang, then we discover, after you git through talkin' 'bout this here other shit, that watchew reeeelly been talkin' 'bout is some other kinda shit! I mean, like got-dammmmmmnnnn!"

Scars and Memories, a large thread on the loom, was supposed to explain the Unexplainable. And it did, for some people. They called me up.

"Now c'mon, Odie, you fulla shit! You talkin' about roaches, rats, basements, stuff like that. And you know damned well that that's some crap you learned about, just like I did, from reading Iceberg Slim and Donald Goines."

In the dream all of this was shown, some of it in black and white. Spike Lee and Robert Townsend would've loved the satire involved.

Scars and Memories purged my writing system. I wouldn't have to worry about dying before the truth about how we had been forced to live was told. Some others had already put their two cents in, now I could say, I've added mine.

In any case, we had decided to stop playing localized tiddlywinks and come off onto another plane. The ghetto writer critics grabbed their balls and headed for the hills.

Their flight was simple and desperate. They, once again, didn't want to be forced to relate to an experience that eclipsed them. Simple as that.

Secret Music. A breath of clear Spring air was sucked in and *Secret Music* exhaled. Now I could begin to explore the collage that exists in every writer's head.

Music, as a thread on the loom, sang sensual songs, vicious songs, daring music, under-water music, crazy stuff.

The feeling of being able to take it all off and dive into ambiotic fluid, a liquid so agreeable to the soul that it was almost impossible to return to the unreal world after the final page was typed.

Menfriends was the last block needed for the dream inspired hexagon. *Menfriends* would force me back to a drawing board that I had left years before, back to the whipping post. But it would also place my head into the position needed for a serious study of myself, and forty or fifty heads like mine.

In duos, trios, quartets, quintets, regiments, they filed through my consciousness. Some of them shook me out of deep sleeps to talk to me, counsel me, rag my ass.

"How come you don't include me in your book, man? I always thought we was tight."

"We always have been tight, Dum Dum, and we always will be. And I do have you in the book but I'm not calling you Dum Dum, I'm calling you by another name."

"Why would you call me by another name when you could call me by my real name?"

"You don't understand, man, each of the men in *Menfriends* is a metaphor for. . . ."

"A metawho?!"

"A metaphor. In other words, each of the dudes really represents, symbolically, some element, or some force, or a principle that I couldn't find a way to talk about except by working through that particular person."

"Don't Dum Dum represent something?"

"Yeah, of course, but like I said, man, I'm using another name for you."

"I still don't see why you couldn't use my real name. I just can't understand why you have to use somebody else's name for me."

"It's complicated, Dum Dum, it's really complicated."

The hexagon was turned slowly, revealing facets of experience that sometimes sparkled like jewels and, at other times, were dull as mud. We played some of the old games, sang a few of the old songs and some of the new ones.

Some of my menfriends died while I wrote about them and returned to haunt me when I got into the second draft. There were others born at the same time.

One sister thought it was, somehow, a bit chauvinistic to be concentrating only on men.

"I mean, where does that place your women friends?"

"In my next book."

SWEET PETER DEEDER

By Odie Hawkins

Peter knew how to pimp by the time he was twelve, taught by his whore mother. She taught him a few other things along the way, things that his friends wouldn't know about until they were much, much older—if ever. Then he was given over to the care of his father, Big Duke. Now Big Duke was not just your average run-of-the-mill pimp. No way. Big Duke was the cock of the walk, with a stable of the best bitches in the city. It was with Big Duke that Peter, the twelve year old Prince, began his *real* education. He was a good student, sharp and fast. By the time he was sixteen Peter was running his high school drug traffic and had himself s string of teenage whores. At eighteen, Peter was a full-fledged pimp and began the long, downward spiral of the drug addict . . . *Sweet Peter Deeder* is, as one critic called it, "An alltogether, getting down masterpiece!"

Personal Sketches of Los Angeles

SECRET MUSIC

BY ODIE HAWKINS

Utilizing the same thrust, power, and formula that made his *Ghetto Sketches* his first bestseller, Odie Hawkins moves the focus from Chicago, where he grew up, to Los Angeles, where he has lived for the past twenty years. And, once again, he has peopled his story with unforgettable characters; there is the telephone freak who drastically changes the lives of several of his victims, bringing ruin to a young virgin, death to a housewife, and happiness to a lonely old woman. Here is a mixed bag of odd lots that only Hawkins could invent. Or does he invent them?

THE BUSTING OUT OF AN ORDINARY MAN

By Odie Hawkins

THE BEST BOOK YET FROM THE BEST-SELLING AUTHOR OF GHETTO SKETCHES, CHILI, CHICAGO HUSTLE AND SWEET PETER DEEDER.

MONDAY EVENING COMIN' DOWN
following the dreariest day of the week anywhere, but especially in the ghetto where people, having taken hangovers and other symptoms of a fast weekend to their individual plantations around town, return to the weight of four (or five) more days of clock punching and lockstepping ahead of them before the eagle flies . . . Here, Odie Hawkins completes what he started in 1972 with *Ghetto Sketches*, the book that placed him in the forefront of black writers. And what he has to say about the main stem is just as pertinent—and explosive—today as it was then! Hawkins has put the fun and games of his last few books aside and gone back to his roots!

SCARS AND MEMORIES: THE STORY OF A LIFE

By Odie Hawkins

Scars and Memories is Odie Hawkins' deeply personal story of his life's journey, from a childhood in Chicago where he was one of the "poorest of the poor" to highly paid Hollywood screenwriter with his own office—and those people, mostly women, who mattered to him along the way. *Scars and Memories* is a tough, gritty book about a survivor who, as a child, lived in dank, cold tenement basements where the cockroaches were so thick on the walls he could set fire to them with rolled up newpapers, where there was seldom enough food, where sex and drugs were as commonplace as summer rain and winter chill. This is a deeply personal story, sometimes painfully told, that only a writer of Hawkins maturity and skill could write. Odie Hawkins is the author of the novels *Chicago Hustle, Chili, The Busting Out of An Orindary Man, Ghetto Sketches* and *Sweet Peter Deeder*

DOPEFIEND
THE STORY OF A BLACK JUNKIE
by DONALD GOINES

Donald Goines is a talented new writer who learned his craft and sharpened his skills in the ghetto slums and federal penitentiaries of America. DOPEFIEND is the shocking first novel by this young man who has seen and lived through everything he writes about. ■ DOPEFIEND exposes the dark, despair-ridden, secret world few outsiders know about—the private hell of the black heroin addict. Trapped in the festering sore of a major American ghetto, a young man and a girl—both handsome, talented, full of promise—are inexorably pulled into the living death of the hardcore junkie. ■ DOPEFIEND is an appalling story because it rings so true. It is also a work of rare power and great compassion. DOPEFIEND will draw you into a nightmare world you will not soon forget.

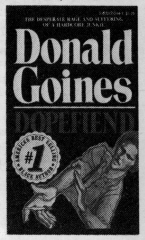

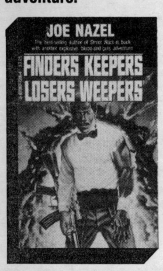

THE BLACK EXPERIENCE FROM HOLLOWAY HOUSE

★ ICEBERG SLIM

AIRTIGHT WILLE & ME (BH269-X)...$2.50
NAKED SOUL OF ICEBERG SLIM (BH713-6)................................2.95
PIMP: THE STORY OF MY LIFE (BH850-7)..................................3.25
LONG WHITE CON (BH030-1)..2.25
DEATH WISH (BH824-8)..2.95
TRICK BABY (BH827-2)..3.25
MAMA BLACK WIDOW (BH828-0)..3.25

★ DONALD GOINES

BLACK GIRL LOST (BH042-5)..$2.25
DADDY COOL (BH041-7)..2.25
ELDORADO RED (BH067-0)..2.25
STREET PLAYERS (BH034-4)..2.25
INNER CITY HOODLUM (BH033-6)..2.25
BLACK GANGSTER (BH263-0)..2.45
CRIME PARTNERS (BH029-8)...2.25
SWAMP MAN (BH026-3)..2.25
NEVER DIE ALONE (BH018-2)..2.25
WHITE MAN'S JUSTICE BLACK MAN'S GRIEF (BH027-1)....2.25
KENYATTA'S LAST HIT (BH024-7)..2.25
KENYATTA'S ESCAPE (BH071-9)..2.25
CRY REVENGE (BH069-7)..2.25
DEATH LIST (BH070-0)..2.25
WHORESON (BH046-8)..2.25
DOPEFIEND (BH044-1)..2.25
DONALD WRITES NO MORE (BH017-4)......................................2.25
   (A Biography of Donald Goines by Eddie Stone)